He's Nothing Like
Them Other Ones

A Novel By
Myiesha

Text **ROYALTY** to 42828

to join our mailing list!

To submit a manuscript for our review, email

us at

submissions@royaltypublishinghouse.com

Text RPHCHRISTIAN to 22828 for our

CHRISTIAN ROMANCE novels!

Text RPHROMANCE to 22828 for our

INTERRACIAL ROMANCE novels!

© 2016

Published by Royalty Publishing House

www.royaltypublishinghouse.com

Chapter 1

Kandi

"I love you, you love me, we're a happy family. With a great big hug and a kiss from me to you, muah," I sang and reached over towards the mirror and kissed my reflection. I was high as kite and loving every minute up. I was 23 years old and in love with a dope dealer named Cali. I was never into drugs until I met him and he introduced me to Venom. Since then, I'd been pumping that stuff in my veins every chance I got. I had all access to it and was able to get high anytime I liked, for free. I looked at myself in the mirror and admired the beautiful image that was me. I had a full caramel face, and thin lips that I had planned on getting bigger. I just had to seduce the money out of Cali. My eyes were my main attraction. I had chinky eyes that would make one think I was mixed with Chinese or some shit, but I wasn't. I was 100% nigger. I stepped back and looked myself over. Although smaller than what I used to be, I was still curvaceous and had a booty that'll make any nigga break their neck to get a peek at. I got it honest from my stuck-up ass momma. I couldn't stand her, but my dick in the booty father was kind of cool. I don't know how my mother couldn't see it, but my father was clearly gay as shit. He had more switch in his hips than she did.

I sat there admiring myself when I heard the front door open and then close. I stripped down naked and looked myself over once again. I opened the drawer of the vanity and pulled out my other favorite drug I called Brittney. I made a line on the table, bent over, and sniffed the line up my nose. I tilted my head up as I let the drug roll down my nostril and into my system. I wiped the remainder that was still on the table, up with my hands, and licked my hands as I made my way downstairs to greet my man.

I was ass naked in nothing but my Steve Madden stilettos and lip gloss. I sashayed down the stairs and into the living room. I was stopped in my tracks when I turned the corner. I don't know if I was tripping because of the drugs or if I was really seeing what I thought I was seeing. Cali was sitting on the couch with a bitch on her knees in front of him, with his dick in her mouth.

"Oh hell motherfucking nah," I said, slurring my words. They both looked up at me.

"Shut the hell up and take yo' ass upstairs," Cali said, at the same time turning the girl's head back around to continue what she was doing.

"Nigga, who the fuck you think you talking to?" I asked, as I proceeded towards them but instead, I tripped over the side table that held the lamp. I was so high I had completely forgot it was there. I landed flat on my titties.

"Bitch, I'm talking to ya junkie ass. Look at you. Can't even see straight yo' ass so high. As a matter of fact, get yo' ass out my shit," Cali said, getting up from the couch, pushing the girl out of his way and headed towards me. He grabbed me by my hair, wrapping it around his hand and yanking my hair until my whole body was moving in a fast direction back out the living room towards the front door. I was clawing at his hands trying to free them from my hair, but I was unsuccessful. I could feel my hair ripping out of my scalp as he pulled me down the hallway. He opened the door and attempted to throw me out the house, but I fought to stay inside that house. I was holding on to the wall for dear life, but I didn't have a good grip. He wrapped his arms around my stomach and picked me up and walked me over to the door. I started fighting, biting, scratching, anything to get myself out of that

9

bear hug he had me in. I didn't understand where all this was coming from. I had no idea why he was throwing me out the way he was. I didn't do anything wrong. I kept his house clean, cooked for him, washed his clothes, I even made sure to sex him as much as possible. What was the reason for him to be treating me like this?

My naked ass hitting the pavement was what brought me out of my thoughts. He had thrown me out on my ass, literally. I got up and ran to the door before he could close it, putting my hand and now bare foot in the doorway, preventing him from closing the door.

"Cali, why are you doing this to me? I was good to you. I done everything you asked of me. Why Cali?" I asked, wiping at my nose.

"You wanna know why, huh? Look at your hand," he said. I looked down at my hand and there was blood on my hand from when I wiped my nose.

"You still wanna know why?" he said, grabbing for my arm and turning it.

'This is why! You're a fucking junkie now. My lady can't be no fucking crackhead. You got so many track marks, New Jersey Transit can ride that shit. Get the fuck away from my house." His harsh words were like daggers. I really couldn't believe him right now. I looked on with tears falling from my eyes.

"Look at yourself, Kandi. You look like a fucking starving Ethiopian, you too damn skinny. I'm sorry, girl, but I can't have you on my arms. Go get yourself some help or something," he said. I looked down at myself. I did lose a bit of weight, but I thought I still looked good.

"Cali, this is your fault. You pumped all that shit in my veins and now you can't rock with me because of something you started. No, Cali, I ain't going no god damn where," I said, attempting to run back inside the house. He tried to shut the door, but I placed my foot in the doorway, completely forgetting that I had no shoes on. The door came slamming against my bare foot so hard it felt like it was just hit with a sledgehammer. I screamed out in pain as I dropped down to the ground, holding my foot.

I was so busy worrying about my foot, I hadn't realized that the front door was now closed. I was sitting outside naked with nothing. I had nothing, no one and nowhere to go. I sat out there banging on the door and calling Cali's name. He was really ignoring my cries, and promises of getting better and not doing drugs anymore. This has been my home for the last year and I wasn't giving up without a fight. I banged on the door so hard that my hands had started to bleed. Now, not only was my foot throbbing, my hands were now in pain.

I sat down on the front stairs, crying and covering my naked body. That's when I remembered that I had went skinny dipping earlier and left the outfit that I had on outside on the beach chair. I stood up and limped around the back to the pool. I opened the gate and walked over to the beach chair, and put on the jean shorts and the tank top. I didn't have any shoes out here, but Cali's Nike slippers were out here, so I slid my feet in the three size too big shoes and started walking out the gate. I got back to the front and looked at the house, realizing that it was over for this. I turned my head and started walking away. I looked at Cali's candy apple Red Audi R8 he had just purchased last week, and got an idea. I picked up one of the bricks that was lining the driveway and walked over to the car. I launched the brick directly into the car, shattering the car window. The alarm went off and I took off down the driveway and out the gate.

Chapter 2

Three Months Later

Kandi

"How much?" a man asked as he pulled up next to me and rolled down his window.

"Twenty-five for head or to fuck. Fifty for both, seventy-five to fuck me in the ass and a hundred for all the above. Pick your poison, baby," I said, running off my Hoe Menu.

"Alright then, get in the car," he said, opening the passenger side door. I slid in and put my seat belt on and directed him to where I was staying. It's been three months since Cali had put me out his house. I needed money and I refused to go to my parents and ask them for anything. Instead, I used what I had to get what I wanted, and what I wanted was drugs. After a few hours of being kicked out, I started getting the itch. When I was with Cali, I was getting high at least every hour. Going five hours without it I thought I was going to die, so I did the only thing I could do. I found

13

one of Cali's workers and offered to give him head for a hit, and he jumped right on it. That only worked for a little while, until he went running his mouth to Cali and Cali told him not to supply me anymore. Since then, I'd been selling myself just to make enough to get high and pay for my stay at the Super 8 motel.

We got out the car and he followed me to my room. I used the key and we walked inside the pissy smelling room. I told him to get ready, while I went and freshened up for him.

After I was done with my whore bath, I came back out into the room and he was lying on the bed ass naked, stroking his hard dick with one hand while the other was behind his head. He was a creepy ass white dude with a serial killer mustache that cover his top lip.

"I see you're up and ready," I said, as I let my silk robe go and revealed my naked body. It wasn't much of a body anymore. The drugs were eating away at me. I had gone from a stacked 140 pounds to 101 pounds at the most. My once beautiful face was dry and sunken in. When I looked in the mirror, I didn't even recognize the person looking back at me, but I still couldn't kick my drug habit.

I walked over to the bed and crawled between his legs. He removed his hand so that I could take him into my mouth. I tried my hardest not to throw up from the smell of his hairy balls. It smelled like sweat mixed with rotten cheese and shit. I tried to just suck the head to avoid going anywhere near his stinky balls, but he kept pushing my head down until I had his whole dick down my throat. I started gagging.

"It's too big for you, baby girl?" he asked. He must have thought I was gagging from the deep throating, but that wasn't it. My deep throating skills were on point. His cheesy smelling balls were what had me on the verge of throwing up.

"Uh huh," I responded.

"Come on, girl, you can't forget about the boys," he said, grabbing a hold of his balls and flapping them. I looked at them and then at him.

"What's that face for, sweet girl?" he asked. I hadn't even realized that I was making a face. If I didn't need to get high, I would have kicked his ass out with the quickness, but I needed the money. I took a deep breath and went down, doing as he asked.

I came back up for air and jumped off the bed. I went over to the desk where my pocketbook sat and started digging through it. I pulled out my small bottle of Majorska and sipped on it, holding some of it in my mouth and swishing it around to get that awful taste out of my mouth. I swallowed it and closed the bottle back, placing it inside my purse. I was about to turn around when I was punched in the side of my head which sent me stumbling towards the door. I didn't know what was going on, but I knew I needed to get my ass up out of here. I grabbed for the doorknob when something tightened around my neck. I grabbed on to what felt like a belt and was trying to stick my hand in between it and my neck, but I couldn't. I tried clawing at his hands, but that too wasn't working. I felt myself start to get light headed from the lack of oxygen I was receiving. I still found the strength to fight back, but he was overpowering me, tossing me around the room while pulling on the belt, tightening it around my neck.

"This what I like," I heard him say as he threw me on the bed onto my stomach. *How is it that I managed to pick up a psycho? This couldn't be my life right now.* He laid his heavy body on top of my frail body. I felt him enter me from behind and started fucking me while pulling on the belt. The tighter the belt got, the faster he started pumping. He pulled out of me and I felt him positioning himself to enter my ass, and I put my hands there to stop him, but he grabbed a hold of my hand and bent it back so far I just knew something was broken. I was scared for my life as I started to slowly lose consciousness. The belt was so tight on my skin I thought my head was going to pop off. He rammed himself inside of me raw, causing complete pain to my ass. Yea, I offered the service to him, but it was at my pace and with lubricant, and I didn't expect to be attacked and damn near choked to death. This was the first and the last time; I was not about this prostituting life anymore. I needed the money, but I needed my life more. He removed the belt from around my neck and pulled out of me, and turned me around onto my back. I took the opportunity to take in as much air as possible, before his hand wrapped around my neck and he started choking me. He placed his penis inside of me and started thrusting inside of me. He was really getting off on this, because the tighter his grip around my neck got, the harder he got, and the deeper he went.

"I'm cumming," he said as he continued to choke and stroke me. He finally let my neck go and rolled off me. I slid down to the floor, trying to catch my breath. I felt something hitting me on the head, but that wasn't my main concern at that point. My concern was staying alive. I got up off the floor and ran and locked myself inside the bathroom.

I sat there on the floor against the door trying to prevent him from coming in and trying to kill me again. I heard the door close and I let out a sigh of relief. I put my hand on my head and cried. I couldn't believe I was just almost killed. I felt something wet and sticky in my hair and I wiped at it. I got up and looked in the mirror. What was hitting my head when I was on the floor was nut. This cracker had bust a nut on my head. Besides being kicked out by Cali, this had to be one of the worst nights of my life. I need to get high; I just prayed that he had at least left the money behind. I slowly opened the door and peeked out. I wanted to make sure he was really gone before I took myself out there. When I made confirmation that the coast was clear, I walked back out and into the room. My eyes lit up when I saw the green paper sitting on the dresser. I ran over to it and picked it up.

"What the fuck?" I yelled looking down at the five-dollar bill. Not only had I almost been killed, I didn't get paid for it either. This was some bullshit. I needed to get high.

Chapter 3

Kandi

It was midnight as I sat in the cut waiting on my victim to come walking by. There were people walking by, but none of them I couldn't take on or overpower. I was on the corner of 33rd and Broadway when I noticed a dollar bus had passed by, and I looked up Broadway to see if anyone had gotten off. There was a girl who looked to be about 18 maybe 19. She was walking towards me with her headphones on and looking down at the phone in her hands. She had her purse on her arms and I figured she would be the perfect target. I ran between the parked cars and ducked down low. I peeked around the car and she was getting closer. I took out my brown paper bag that I had cutout eyes and a mouth, and placed it over my head. I waited until she walked by me and I ran up on her. I grabbed her phone out her hand and her purse off her arm, as I did the crackhead run up towards the park. I ran so fast I don't think my feet were even touching the ground. I don't know where I got the speed from, but I think it was the drugs and the determination to get high that turned

19

me into Olympic track star, Sanaya Richards.

When I got into the park, I ran and hid behind the bushes, removing the paper bag mask. I unzipped the pocketbook and poured out everything inside the bag. I used the light from the phone and started rummaging through it, looking for anything I could make a profit from. There wasn't shit in here but makeup, gum, lotion, a lighter, and a wallet that only had an ID inside and full of nothing but pennies.

"Shit," I yelled, disappointed that I had just done all that for nothing. As I was picking all the stuff up and putting it back inside the bag, something caught my eyes. A smile spread across my face and I picked it up and examined it. Indeed, it was a blunt. I was used to the stronger drugs, but I guess this could do a little something. I used the lighter and sparked it up. I sat there smoking on the blunt as I thought of my next move.

After a few pulls, I realized that it wasn't doing shit for me. Just then I noticed spot lights from a police car coming my way. I laid down on the ground and waited for it to pass. When it did, I grabbed the cell phone and my paper bag mask, crawled out and crackhead dodged through the park. With no destination in mind, I just ran until I couldn't run anymore. I sat down on the curb to catch my breath. I pulled the blunt and lighter out and continued puffing on the blunt. I looked around the neighborhood realizing that the area was familiar to me. I turned around and how fucking ironic it was that I ended up in front of Cali's house. I stood up and walked over the gate and looked up the driveway. His car wasn't there and the lights were out. I climbed over the short gate, ducking low as I ran up the driveway and around to the back of the house. I pulled out my trusty brown paper bag mask and placed it over my head, and I reached for the doorknob, praying that Cali still had a habit of leaving this door unlocked; and he did.

I slowly and quietly walked into the house, making sure to not alert anyone of my presence. Three months and this house still looked exactly the same. I walked up the stairs slowly. If I remembered correctly, the stairs squeaked when you stepped in certain spots. I knew Cali had some expensive watches and jewelry that I could sell and get a lot of money for. I walked down the hallway until I was standing at Cali's room door. I opened it and walked in. The room was dark and I didn't want to cut the lights on, just in case someone had pulled up and seen the light on, it would give me away. I went straight to the bathroom where he kept his jewelry box. I quietly shut the door and turned on the light. "Jackpot," I said quietly, walking over to the vanity where his black jewelry box sat. I opened it and started stuffing my pockets with his platinum chains, Rolex and diamond earrings. When my pockets were full, I shut it back and was about to walk out the bathroom, when I remembered my stash that I kept in the bathroom under the sink. I opened the cabinet and reached under, finding my prize. I was shocked it was still there, but then again, we never kept anything down there, and apparently they still didn't. I pulled out the tin container that had all the tools I needed. I pulled the shower door open and climbed inside and shut the door back. I pulled out the spoon, the needle, the rock and the lighter, and prepared for my high. Two minutes later, I was tying the band around my arm and searching for a vein. When I was able to locate it, I plunged the needle in and injected the Venom into my body. I was beyond high and I wasn't sure if I would or when I was coming down.

"Draya, bring yo' ass in here." I was awakened by Cali's voice. I jumped up, looking around, trying to remember where I was.

"What, baby? What happened?" a female asked as she entered the bathroom.

"What the fuck I tell yo' ass about leaving these fucking

lights on, huh?" Cali asked, followed by the sound of a slap.

"Do yo' ass pay any bills around this bitch?"

Slap!

"I swear I cut them off, Cali," the girl cried.

"So then how the fuck they get back on then, huh? What you telling me, Casper the friendly ghost cut the shits on? The wind blew them on?" I sat there listening to Cali's cheap ass smack the girl around over some fucking lights. I held back my laugh, because the shit was hysterical to me. He was still a cheap ass motherfucker, but one thing for sure, he never smacked my ass around like that until the night he put me out.

When he was done, the girl ran out the bathroom crying as I listened to the sound of Cali pissing. I silently started counting down from five waiting for it. Cali always had a habit of farting during his piss and like I expected, he farted. I held on to my mouth trying to prevent myself from laughing out loud. He flushed the toilet and walked out the bathroom, cutting the light off. Nasty fuck ain't even wash his hands.

I waited a little longer before quietly climbing out the

shower. I walked over to the bathroom door and listened out. It was silent and after looking under the door, it was dark inside the room. I opened the door and crawled out on my hands and knees into the dark room that was filled with the sounds of Cali snoring. The moonlight helped me get through the room and to the door safely. I started getting excited the closer I got to the door just from the thought of how much cash I was about to get from all Cali's jewelry that I had in my pocket.

"You put your trust in a nigga, stupid hoe, how you figure he won't fuck your best friend and your sister" The sound of Khia's song "Don't Trust No Nigga" came blaring from somewhere. I stopped in my tracks as I felt the vibration in my pocket from the girl's phone that I had stolen. I pulled it out and tried to quickly cut the ringer off before Cali woke up, but it was too late. He sat up in the bed like Michael Myers. I dropped the phone right there and said fuck it, as I climbed to my feet and proceeded to run out the room.

"What the fuck?" I heard Cali say as I started running down the hall. I was right at the edge of the stairs when I felt someone kick me in the ass and I went tumbling head first down the hard ass stairs. It felt like I was tumbling forever before I came to a stop at the bottom of the landing. I got up and tried running towards the door, but I was getting nowhere fast. The pain from my ankle every time I came down on it was preventing me from moving at crackhead speed. I must've twisted it during the tumble down the stairs.

"I'll teach you motherfuckers for breaking in my house," I heard Cali say from behind me.

I was almost at the door when I heard a loud boom and I felt a stinging pain in my back. I fell to the floor, unable to move. I felt Cali walking up behind me and he turned my frail, 90-pound body over with his foot.

"Ah shit, Kandi," he said looking down at me as I lie on the floor bleeding.

"Fuck yo' crackhead ass doing in my house?" I tried to speak but no words were coming out. He looked down at my pockets and bent down and started emptying them out.

"Yo' ass was about to rob my ass blind, right? I should leave yo' ass right here to die. Draya, bring my keys downstairs," Cali yelled up the stairs to the female he had just got finish smacking around, no more than two hours ago. Minutes later, he was picking me up and carrying me outside to his car. The girl opened up the door and Cali threw me in the back on to the floor. Like literally threw me on to the floor of the back seat. The nigga ain't even have the decency to lay me on the backseat. I mean what I was expecting? I did just try and rob this man's house.

I felt myself becoming weak. I wasn't sure if it was from the amount of blood I was losing or a delayed high from the drugs, but whatever it was I knew it couldn't be good. I wasn't sure where Cali was taking me and I was scared for my life. I tried to stay awake, but I slowly felt my conscious start to slip away.

Chapter 4

2 years later

Kandi

"So you think you can dance?" June, the owner of Velour, asked me as I stood there in front of him in nothing but boy shorts and a cheetah print bustier.

"I can do a little something," I responded with a smile.

"Cool, show me what you got," June said, looking me up and down. I turned and sashayed away, making my way over to the pole. I stepped up on stage and waited for the music to start playing.

"I'm calling ya daddy (daddy)
Can you be my daddy (daddy)
I need a daddy (daddy)
Won't you be my daddy (daddy)

Come and make it rain down on me
Come and make it rain down on me..."

Twista's "Wetter" song started playing as I grabbed on to the pole and walked around it. I came back around to the front and faced my audience. I leaned against the pole as I seductively wound my body to music. I squatted down and now had my legs wide open, so they could get a peek of my fat kitty poking through my underwear. June looked at me with so much lust in his eyes I just knew I had the job in the bag. I dropped down into split and bounced up and down, as my ass cheeks made smacking sounds on the stage floor.

It's been two years since I had last used any form of drugs. After the night I was attacked and shot in the back, I promised myself and God that if I had survived that night I was going to get clean, and that's what I did. That night, Cali had dropped me off at the hospital. He literally pushed me out of the car in front of the emergency room, and he pulled off leaving me to be found by the next person to walk out the door. I had lost a lot of blood, but my reason for passing out that night was from the drugs. After I was discharged from the hospital, I was admitted into a rehab center to help me kick my heroin addiction. It took me a while, but I had finally did it. During the two years, I gained all my weight back plus more. I was back to being thick and curvy like I liked it. My skin had cleared up from the dark patches that invaded my skin, and my hair had started to grow again. If you knew me then and compared me to now, you would have thought I was two different people.

I got up off the floor and walked over to June and started teasing him a little. I climbed on top of him and straddled his lap, as I started grinding my pelvis on his lap. I climbed off, put my hands on my knees, and started bouncing my ass up and down, jiggling my booty on his kneecaps. I got down on my hands and knees and turned and laid on my back. I lifted my legs straight up in the air and then spread them wide, giving him a clear view of my vagina. I grabbed on to my left leg and pulling it over my head. With my leg still stretched over my head, I rolled over from my back and into another split. I was about to transition into my next move when the music stopped and June gave me a standing ovation.

"You really do have some moves I see," June said, helping me off the floor.

"Yup, so do I have the job?" I anxiously asked. He sat there silently looking me up and down.

"How bad do you want the job?"

"I really need this job," I answered.

"Ok, follow me," he said, waving me to the back. I heard the guy he was sitting at the table with laugh, and I turned and looked at him. He smiled and winked at me. I wasn't sure what that was for, but I continued to follow June to the back.

When we got in his office, he sat behind his desk with his hands folded against his chin.

"How old are you Kandi Kane?"

"I'm 25."

"Nice," he said getting up out of his chair. He walked around the desk and over to me. "How bad do you need this job?" he asked me, coming up behind me and moving my hair to the side. I moved over so that I was now standing on the side of him. He walked back over to me.

"I really need this job. Even if it's not this job, I'll wash glasses if I have to."

"Nah, you'll be perfect as a dancer, Kandi Kane. Besides, they make the most money. There's just one thing," he said grabbing a hold of my hand and bringing it to his lips and kissing it.

"What is it? Application, submit a drug test, just tell me and I'll get it done. What do I have to do?" I asked. He walked closer to me, wrapped his arms around my waist and pulled me closer to him.

"If you want me to give you a job, you have to do something for me." I knew exactly what he meant by the look in his eyes. I had a thought to just walk up out of here, but my feet wouldn't move. It's been two years since I traded sex for money. I wasn't trying to go back to that life, but I needed this job. I've filled out applications at fast food restaurants, pet stores, supermarkets, even at a gas station, and no one wanted to hire me.

I felt June's hands start to slide down my boy shorts and he squeezed my ass. Once he saw that I wasn't resisting, he continued, moving his hands further under my ass until his fingers was at the opening of my vagina. He pushed them in and I moaned out in pain. I had been abstinent for two years and it felt like I was a virgin again.

"You like that, Kandi Kane?" he asked me, as his finger slid in and out of me. I didn't answer him; I just sat quietly as he continued to fondle me.

31

"You're so tight, Kandi Kane. Come over here and let daddy June get a taste of that thing," he said, pulling me over to the desk. He bent me over a little as he slid my underwear down. He was behind me, so I had no idea what he was doing, that was until I felt his mouth on vagina. I closed my eyes, trying to disappear from the uncomfortable situation.

"Damn, girl, you taste like a chocolate covered strawberry. You certainly have the right name," he said, standing up. I heard him fumbling with his belt as I felt his hot breath on my neck. *Father, please forgive me,* I silently prayed as I felt June anxiously drop his pants and pull out his small dick.

"Bend all the way over, girl. Let me get this thing in there," he said. I laughed to myself. That was the only way he was going to get it in there. His dick was so small there was probably no other position that worked for him.

"Can you put a condom on please?" I asked him. With his pants around his ankles, he shuffled around to his desk and pulled out a condom and placed it on his little pecker, then shuffled back over to me. I wanted to get this over with, so I bent over like I was asked and started counting to 100. That was one of my relaxation techniques I picked up in rehab. I felt him get really close up on me and then he started thrusting himself into me. I wasn't sure what he was doing, but I guess he thought he was doing something.

"Ah shit, girl, you feel so good," he moaned. I looked around a little confused.

"Shit," he said again. That's when I realized that he was already inside of me and about 20 seconds from nutting. He was inside of me and I ain't even know it. This man really needed to start looking into some penile enlargement procedures because this was just sad. His fingers hurt more when they went inside of me then his little ass dick. A whole minute later he was done, and he flopped down on his pleather couch. I turned around and pulled my underwear back up. I looked down at him as he stroked his little shrimpy penis.

"Where is the condom?" I asked, looking around for the condom, but it was nowhere in sight.

"Girl, don't worry about that, I'm safe. You won't catch nothing," he said, sounding dumb as he looked.

"Oh yea, is that what you tell all the girls that give you a little something for a job?" I asked him. He just sat there trying to catch his breath.

"You start tomorrow. Now get out my office so I can get some sleep," he said. I looked at him and thought about busting him in the head with the stapler that was on his desk. I turned and walked out the door. I was going to make sure first thing tomorrow morning to hit up Planned Parenthood and get tested.

Chapter 5

5 Years Later

John

"We're going to the ship, we're going to the ship," my team cheered while in the locker room. We had just won the play-offs and were headed to the championship game. During my free time, I coached the Paterson All- Stars Jr. Pee Wee basketball team.

"Ok, the game ball goes to..." I said as the team did a drum roll, waiting for me to say a name.

"My main man, Kianni," I said as everyone started clapping.

"Twenty points this game, that's amazing, little man," I said, rubbing the top of his head and handing him the game ball.

"That's momma's superstar right there," his mother yelled from the back of the room. I looked over at her and smiled.

Kianni's mother was bad as shit. I told myself that one day I would gain the courage to talk to her. Seeing as though she was a few years older than me, I was a little scared she would shoot me down.

"Coach John, you still treating us to Pizza Hut like you promised?" one of my boys asked.

"That's what I said, right, knuckle head? I always keep my promise. Now, everyone go change so we can go fill our bellies with some pizza." They all started to scurry to get changed as the parents and the coaches waited outside.

"You know today was the first time I have ever really heard you speak," I said to Kianni's mother.

"Well, that's because I don't typically have much to say to anyone. I speak when I'm spoken to, and today I was just excited about the team winning the game," she said.

"What's your name again? I don't want to keep calling you Kianni's mom."

"It's Kandice," she answered.

"That name is perfect for you."

"Oh yea, how so?"

"It's a beautiful name for a beautiful woman. Are you coming out for pizza with us, Kandice?" I asked her.

"Nah, I have to be to work in a few hours," she answered.

"Come on, don't be a party pooper. Besides, this was Kianni's game, let him celebrate." I can tell she really didn't want to, but she knew I was right.

"Alright. We can go just for a little while, but then we have to go," she said. We waited five more minutes before the boys excitedly stormed out of the locker room. We all piled into our personal cars and made our way to Pizza Hut. While everyone was there mingling and the boys were over by the video games, Kandice, like always, sat there quietly. I couldn't keep my eyes off of her. She was beautiful, but something with her was off. As the parents continued their conversation, I got up and went and sat in Kianni's chair next to Kandice.

"So what you doing working at night? How does your husband feel about you not being home at nights?" I asked her, trying to get to know her and at the same time, pulling the information I wanted out of her.

"I know damn well you don't see a ring on this finger," she

37

said, causing me to laugh because she was on to me.

"Ok, so how does your man feel about that?"

"He's fine with it. He knows momma has to get this money."

"He should be getting that money for you while you lay your head peacefully at night."

"Yea, well, I'm sure if he was of age he would, but I doubt if he could get a job at five years old," she said, making me laugh, at the same time, reviving my chances with her.

"I get it, you're one of those 'my son is my King' moms, huh?"

"Yes, because he is. I live for him, provide for him, and I will die for him," she said.

"Nah, Ma, I get it. So what is it that you do?" I asked her. She looked around then smiled.

"I'm a stripper," she answered. I laughed at her, not believing a word she said.

"Yea, whatever, it's ok, you don't have to answer me. I would really like to take you out one day," I said.

"I don't think that'll happen, but I really enjoyed myself.

It's about time for Kianni and I to get going," she said, getting out of her chair.

"Ok, well it was nice talking to you Kandice; I guess I'll see you at the next game."

"Enjoy your night, Coach John," she said as she walked over to Kianni and they left out the door. I couldn't help but watch her ass as she walked out the restaurant.

"So what's shorty's story?" my brother, Tech, asked.

"I don't know yet, but I'll find out," I said with confidence.

"Nigga, she's probably twice ya age. Something about her lips look familiar as hell." I shook my head at him. Every chick that walked passed looked familiar to him.

"That shit doesn't mean anything. Age ain't nothing but a number; besides, I don't look nor do I act like ya average 25-year-old."

"And how does an average 25-year-old act?" Tech asked. I turned and looked him up and down.

"Like you, bitch."

"Forget you, nigga. Ya ole Similac ass ain't got a chance with that grown ass woman. You might as well stick to these young broads out here that's flinging them kitty cats at you left and right."

"Yea, that's exactly why I don't want them. They're quick to sling them coochies to any money making nigga in Paterson. I need me a woman like that one that just walked up out of here, and not some little girl. I'm bringing in close to half a mil a year, I have my own. I need me a wife to help me build my kingdom, a young chick wouldn't know how to do that."

"I hear you, nigga, but what's going on with that nigga, Cali?" Tech asked.

"Man, I don't know what the fuck is up with that nigga. He gotta be high on some kind of shit for his pussy ass to step to me on some shit. I should have deaded that nigga for even thinking I would steal anything. I don't work for him; this shit we got going on is a partnership. Without each other, we both don't make no money," I said, feeling myself becoming bothered by the situation that happened earlier today. Cali was the local kingpin around here. He had a custom strand of heroin that he called Venom, and everyone around the world wanted their hands on the drug. That's where I came in. I owned my own charter bus company. It brought in money, but

I wanted more. Cali approached me on a business deal that I couldn't turn down. This nigga offered me 20 grand per trip to use my bus to transport his product across state lines undetected. Once his men loaded the product into the flooring of the bus, it was my job to make sure it made it safely, and 10 times out of 10 it did. The last shipment was missing a few keys when it was dropped off, and Cali had the nerve to come out his mouth on some other shit. He was two seconds from deep throating my gun. I trusted my employees and if I ever had to question them, I had cameras to do so. The fact that he was questioning them meant that he was questioning me. If anybody needed to be questioned, it was his snake ass. Before he became head nigga in charge, he worked for Previous, who was well known and a well-respected man. Not only was he respected for his dealings, but for his generosity. Every month, he held dinners for the city; during Christmas, he gave out Toys R Us gift cards to parents to ensure that the kids had a decent holiday. He started the basketball team and after a while, he passed it over to me for me to run. Previous' sudden passing was a big mystery to everyone. That man was in perfect health and had no enemies, and he just dropped dead and left his drug business to a snake like Cali. Something wasn't right at all. I was going to make it my personal business to find out.

"Word, I had my hand on the burner waiting for your cue, my nigga. You blast, I blast, that's the motto, motherfucker."

"And that's why when I eat, you eat. You had my back from jump. I appreciate that shit, man."

"Nigga, are you fucking kidding me? You took my homeless ass in when I ain't have a place to go. You begged your parents to let me stay there. If anything, I owe you. I appreciate you letting a nigga eat and all by keeping my pockets fat, but you don't owe me shit. Holding you down is the least I can do," Tech said, giving me dap.

My mother and father adopted Tech when he was 12 years old. He and I had been friends for a while before I discovered he had no home. I had found him sleeping inside one of the tunnels in the jungle gym at the park. I had called myself running away one night because my mother took my game system away from me because of a bad report card. I got mad and packed my book bag with my game controller, two pairs of boxers, and my Undertaker wrestling man, and ran out the house. I didn't go far; I just went around the corner to the park, where I found Tech balled up inside of the tunnel sleeping. I sat there with him, making sure not to wake him. I assumed my parents would come looking for me sooner or later, but they never came. It started raining and the wind started blowing, and I couldn't take it anymore. I looked over at Tech who was shivering from the cold, and I woke him up. I told him to come home with me where it was warm and dry. I was so mad when I got to the house. The cars were still parked in the driveway, the porch light was off, and the door was unlocked. These mofos didn't even bother to come look for me. They were cozied away in the bed when I peeked into their bedroom.

Tech and I went to my bedroom. I made him a bed on the floor with my Ninja Turtle blankets, and gave him some of my clothes to change into. The next morning when I woke up and went downstairs to get us bowls of cereal, my parents had already had a breakfast spread on the table. They asked if I was going to invite my friend downstairs. When he came downstairs, he ate like he had never eaten before. My parents noticed how starved he was and started asking about his living situations. He lied, but after I told them where I found him sleeping, they started looking into it more and discovered that he was a ward of the state and had run away from his foster home. When my parents went to return him back to the foster home, he ran away from them. My dad, whose side job was a bounty hunter, was able to track Tech down and when he found him, he had a deep conversation with him. I later found out that he had opened up to my father about his foster father touching him in ways that made him feel uncomfortable. My father being from an abusive home was bothered by the situation and felt for the kid, so he and my mom adopted Tech. A few weeks after, Tech's foster father was found floating in the Passaic River. His death was ruled a suicide but still to this day, something is telling me my father had something to do with that suicide. My parents adopted Tech and ever since, he's been my brother and best friend. Just thinking about my mother almost brought tears to my eyes.

"Nigga, let's get ready to get up out of here," I said, stretching out my arms.

"What you mean? You still got about twenty pies that ain't been touched yet," Tech said.

"Yea, I'm dropping those off to Sister Pat at the shelter. You know I gotta keep Previous' tradition alive 'cause that fuck boy, Cali, don't give back shit. That's the least he could do. After all, he's faithfully littering the street with drugs."

"Word. That nigga stingier than a motherfucker. I got plans for his ass," Tech said. I just shook my head because

Tech was always up to something.

"What you doing tonight?" I asked him.

"Shit, might go see what's shaking at Velour."

"Dude, you know what's shaking at Velour. Titties and ass like always."

"Exactly. I need to get slapped in the face by an ass cheek or a titty," he said, making me laugh.

"Aight. Don't say shit when one of those dirty girls slap a crab or yeast on ya face, nasty ass."

"Shut up, 'cause nigga, you coming right along with me. So be ready, bitch, and have some singles for my girls. They work very hard. It ain't easy pussy popping on a hand stand for the pleasure of us niggas. Respect the hoes, aight?" he said, getting up and leaving. I gathered all the kids and parents up, paid the bill, and we all departed the restaurant. I had the staff bring the twenty pies out to my car. I tipped them and made my way to the shelter.

Chapter 6

Kandi

"By any means necessary, Kianni will eat. By any means, Kianni will have the world," I said as I coached myself in the dressing room mirror. I had been working in this hell hole for the past 5 years, and I was always two seconds from walking straight out the fucking door. I couldn't stand this place, but my son needed to eat and this was the easiest thing to come by. The money I made was on point, but I couldn't stand most of these young bitches in here, and especially that fucking bastard, June. Just thinking of him made my blood boil. I picked up the double shot of Henny and threw it back, then finished putting on the rest of my performance outfit. I was performing as a sexy firefighter routine tonight. I was going on stage in a few, so I decided to give my little man a call before I went on, although I knew he would be sleeping. Just as I was about to hit the call button on my screen, the dressing room door came open and immediately, my skin began to crawl. I looked up at him with disgust as he walked over to my chair. At that moment, I wished I wasn't in this room alone, unlike other times when I prayed no one else was in this room with me.

"Mm, mm, mm," he said as walked over to my chair and stood above me. I ignored him as I opened up Kianni's Pokémon Go game and started checking for Pokémon. I told Kianni I would keep an eye out for him. He was in a competition with his friend Joey from school.

"How's my baby momma doing?" he asked, causing me to throw up in my mouth. I looked around the room checking to see if there was anyone else in the room with us.

"You must be talking to your reflection because you ain't got no baby momma up in here. You made that perfectly clear five years ago," I said, catching an immediate attitude with him. This fucker really did get on my fucking nerves.

"Aww, come on, Kandi. Don't be like that. I'm sorry. I had to do what I had to do. I'm a married man and you coming at me talking about you pregnant, I can't have that. If my wife was to find out, she would divorce my ass and take everything

I own, including my club. I couldn't have that, Kandi Kane," he said, reaching down to touch my cheek, but I moved my face out the way.

"June, shut ya black ass up and get the hell up out of my face with the bullshit, because I don't give a flying fuck about you, your wife, or ya club. You're worried about her all of sudden, because clearly you weren't thinking about your wife or this hell hole of a club the night you took that condom off? Did you think I wanted to get pregnant by yo' ass? No the fuck I didn't. Even when I asked you to give me the money to get an abortion, yo' ass couldn't even do that. I could take yo' ass to child support and there were plenty of times I thought about doing so, but I came to the conclusion that I don't want yo' ass in my son's life. You're no fucking father to him, so don't ever open yo' mouth to even refer to him as your baby. Fuck outta here," I said, pushing my chair back so hard that it connected with his stomach and damn near knocked the wind out of him. I grabbed my costume hat and left out the room.

John

I pulled up to the club around 11:30. After I had dropped the pizza off at the shelter, I went home to shower and I ended up falling asleep. Tech had been blowing my phone up for the past hour. When I pulled up, he was standing outside talking to a bunch of niggas. I had no idea who they were. Maybe they were all regulars like my brother's perverted ass.

I parked my car and jumped out.

"Yurrp," I called over to Tech who turned around and looked.

"About fucking time, nigga. It's some hot ass in there and they were starting to get cold messing with yo' ass," he said, giving me dap as I stepped on the sidewalk. Him and I proceeded inside the club. When we got in there, the music was blasting and colorful spot lights were circulating around the room. On stage, there were two strippers standing inside of a kiddie pool. One was a redhead in a blue two-piece outfit and the other was a blonde in a pink two-piece outfit. They both were cute, but neither one aroused me not even a bit.

"Oh shit, we're just in time for the Honey Bowl. Come on, nigga, let's take our seats," Tech said, pulling my arm like a little excited ass kid about to watch a movie. When we got to our tables in the VIP section, there was bottles on ice and appetizers and shit.

"T, man, what the hell you got all this liquor for just the two of us?" I asked him.

"Because it's not just the two of us. Teddy and Dre on their way, too. Just like yo' ass, they running late. I don't know why ya niggas can't ever make it to places in a timely, respectable fashion. Y'all think everybody has to run on y'all time, right?" he said, picking up a chicken wing. I wanted to laugh, but he was really being serious. I don't know what it was about this nigga and time. He was forever watching the clock, forever beasting about niggas running late, he kept a watch on at all times, and had a clock installed in every room of his house, even in his fucking shower.

"Calm yo' ass down and watch ya Honey Bowl," I said, while dipping a celery stick inside of the ranch dressing.

"Yo, yo, yo," I heard Dre say from behind us. I turned, and him and Teddy were walking up to the table. I stood up and greeted them both.

"What up, Teddy Bear?" I asked Teddy, as I pinched one of his nipples like I have always been doing since teenagers.

"Nigga, I told yo' ass about doing that shit. I'm going to eat ya ass one day. Uncle Darius will be missing a son," he said. Teddy hated when I pinched his nipples but I couldn't help it.

I told that nigga it was time for him to go on a diet; he was starting to need a bra. Teddy was 6'1 and had to be around 350 pounds of all fat, and he refused to go on a diet. Me and my father, who they all referred to as Uncle Darius, have been trying to get him to start exercising, but dude was so lazy. The first thing he did when he got to the table was pull the platter of chicken wings in front of him and he went in.

Dre on the other hand was more low-key, more chilled. He didn't speak much unless he was spoken to, and when he did speak, he was always dropping some knowledge on us niggas. Dude was smart as hell. He was more of a listener than a speaker, so all he did was absorb new shit in every day. He was close with my father who was also a very smart man, and when he got around my father, he and my father would talk for hours about politics and Wall Street kind of shit. Dre was a smart kid, but dumb at the same time. Instead of him using his brain and implementing it into positives things, he chose to run the streets. I blame myself for that, too, because he looked up to me as well, and my life was all about the streets. I wasn't raised in the streets nor was I raised in the hood, but I stayed there so much, the streets became a part of me. I respected my father, but I looked up to Previous. Previous taught me the game, and about the streets and the drugs. That's why when it was said that he gave everything to fucking Cali, that shit was a big ass mystery to me.

"Let's get ready to Honey Bowl," the emcee yelled into the mic. When he did, both girls went after each other attempting to slam each other down into the pool full of honey. The shit was more funny than erotic. They were able to have secret weapons they were able to bring out on stage—nothing that could cause harm, but little things to increase the funny.

By the end of the fight, the redhead had the blonde face down in the honey and was sitting on top of her back, bouncing up and down. She climbed out the pool, went to the back, and came back out with a bucket of blue feathers and threw them all over her honey covered opponent. She looked like a big ass human size blue bird. The audience was laughing as the men walked up and started throwing money on stage. Both girls collected their money and exited the stage.

"Alright, alright. How ya feeling tonight?" the emcee asked. The other staff hurriedly cleared and cleaned the stage.

"That was some great entertainment, right fellas and wannabe fellas?" he laughed, while pointing to the studs in the front row.

"Pepper was wrong for covering ole girl in feathers. That was downright cold. Well let's set this place on fire because coming to the stage is the sexist firefighter any of you have ever laid eyes on. Give it up for everyone's favorite, the showstopper herself. Y'all know who I'm talking about, right?"

"Kandi, Kandi, Kandi," the crowd started shouting, whistling, banging on the tables. I, on other hand, had no idea what or who they were talking about. Even Tech, Dre, and Teddy were shouting for some Kandi. Next thing I know, I was getting popped in the head with shit. I looked down on the table and it was filled with candy. It was raining fucking Nerds, Laffy Taffy, and Blow Pops. This Kandi dancer was a big deal. I almost couldn't wait for the show to start. Horns and sirens started going off and the lights dimmed. My eyes were now glued to the stage. The music started playing and I was even more intrigued. Baby girl was about to get busy to some hood shit.

"I'm a smoke this joint then I'm a break you off,

I be lying if I said you ain't the one.

All these tattoos in my skin they turn you on.

Lotta smoking drinking that's the shit I'm on.

Heard you not the type that you take home to mom.

Is we fucking when we leave the club or nah..."

Ty Dolla Sign's song "Or Nah" started playing, and a sexy ass firefighter walked out on stage. I couldn't take my eyes off her ass that poked out from under that short, red fireman coat. The graceful way her hips swayed had my full attention. Her red, leather boots came all the way up, suffocating her thick thighs, and she had some sexy candy red lips that poked out from under her hat. I couldn't see her face because of how low her hat was pulled down. When she got to the center stage, she opened up her jacket and had on a red pleather two-piece set. She started winding her body sensually as she leaned against the pole. She dropped down into a squat while completely removing her jacket and throwing it to one of the bouncers in front of the stage. This girl really had to be something else, because they didn't have bouncers surrounding the stage for any of the other dancers, but she had about four guarding the stage.

She opened up her legs wide enough to give us a clear view of her clean, neatly shaven kitty. My mouth started watering and it felt like my tongue had just rolled out of my mouth and onto the floor. Once she felt like she had given the crowd a good enough view, she dropped down into a split, then brought her leg around, bouncing into another split in the opposite direction, now giving us a view of that fat ass. You could hear the sound of her ass cheeks hitting the stage. Her ass looked like two nicely golden, buttery biscuits, and I was about ready to take a big bite out of that shit.

By the end of her show, just like all the rest of the niggas up in here, I was sitting there stunned, staring at an empty ass stage. Ma did what she had to do and bounced on our ass. The crazy part was, not once did she take her hat off so I had no idea what she looked like. The even crazier part is that during the performance, you weren't allowed to throw money; these niggas had the nerve to send around a fucking collection plate. All the niggas in here were in a trance and putting all the money they had inside the damn collection plate. She had to have collected at least 20 thousand tonight, but shawty's performance was well worth it and I must say she had a new fan.

"Alright, alright niggas, close y'all mouths before a fly, fly in those shit boxes," the emcee said, coming back onstage, knocking everyone out their trances. Niggas started getting up and leaving and after checking my pockets, I was two seconds from being right behind them. I knew I dropped a stack up in that damn collection plate. That was more than I planned on spending. I walked over to the stage to one of the bouncers.

"Big Mike, what's up with you, homie?" I asked him as we bumped fists.

"Shit, man, just working hard, trying to be like you," he said.

"Man, you too old to try and be like me, try and be better, it's never too late. I have a question, that girl that was just on stage, what's her deal?" I asked and he started laughing.

"Why, you feeling her?" he asked.

"Maybe."

"That's Kandi. She's one of the specials around here. She's quiet, she fucks with no one, and no one dares to fuck with her. I had to stop her from beating a couple bitches' asses up in here. She's a sweet girl, though."

"What she look like under that hat?" I asked.

"She's beautiful, man. If an angel had a face it'll be Kandi's face. If Honey Nut Cheerios had a face, it'll be her face. If Wendy's 4 for 4 deal had a face, it'll be her face. That woman is gorgeous and definitely does not need to be up in here working for June's sheisty ass."

"Yo' fat ass just had to bring up food, right?" I said, laughing at him.

"You damn right, because food is beautiful to me and so is Kandi. But let me get my ass back to work. Aye, maybe you should go find her, the two of you would look good together. She needs a nigga like you to show her the finer things in life, take her away from all this shit," Big Mike said, walking off. How the hell was I supposed to find someone and I had no idea what she looked like?

Turning to leave, I swiped a box of the strawberry Nerds off the table and left out the club.

It was going on three in the morning when everyone started leaving the club. That red-head dancer, Pepper, was talking with Tech, or should I say they were over there dry fucking against the wall. Pepper was a cute girl. Bright red hair, tanned caramel complexion, tall, long legs, and nice, toned, fit body.

"Y'all take that shit to the telly, my nigga," Teddy yelled

over to the two of them.

"Ignore that nigga, he's always coming up with great ideas," Tech said with a cheesy grin on his face.

"That doesn't sound like a bad idea. We can save that money and just go to my place," the stripper said.

"Well, let's go then," Tech said, wrapping his arm around Pepper.

"Here, nigga," I said, digging inside my wallet and pulling out a Magnum and throwing it at him; he caught it.

"Thanks, bro, but I'm covered," he said as they both jumped inside his metallic blue 2016 Camaro RS. I sat there on top of my car going through my phone as I partially listened to Teddy and Dre's conversation. Teddy started telling us about his last experience with a stripper. He was explaining how he let a stripper turn him into a S'more, which got my full attention, because I needed to know how this turned out. He let her spread Fluff, the marshmallow spread, all over him, and then she melted chocolate on his stomach and started scooping it with Graham crackers. She then tied him to bed, stole all his money, and left him looking like the Michelin man. I laughed so hard I damn near fell off the hood of my car. The shit men will go through for some pussy.

"Aight, I'm about to get going. I'll catch you bums later," I said, waving bye and getting inside my car. I rolled down the windows and pulled out of the parking spot. Before exiting the parking lot, I stopped and was looking for some music to bump to as I took my drive home. As I was searching, I heard someone having trouble starting their car. At first I ignored it, but the constant turning of the engine made me look up. I couldn't believe my eyes when I looked up.

Chapter 7

Kandi

"Shit," I cursed as I got out of my car. I walked around to the front of my dead car. I popped the hood of my car like I knew what I was doing when in fact I had no idea. I stood there with my hands on my hips, feeling hopeless. My 2004 Honda Accord has been hanging with me for the last five years, and she has been giving me trouble for the last two years, but she always managed to not let me down.

"Come on, baby girl, don't give up on momma. I promise I'll take you to the waterpark first thing tomorrow if you behave," I said, rubbing at the side of my car.

"You can try giving it a kiss, that always works for me," I heard someone say behind me. I hesitated before turning around. When I did turn around, I became slightly uncomfortable.

"Coach John, how are you?" I asked, pulling the hood of my Pink sweat suit jacket over my head.

"I'm good, Miss Kandice, how are you?"

"It's Kandice, please don't call me Miss, makes me feel old."

"Sorry, definitely don't want to do that. Would you like for me to take a look at it for you?"

"Uh, no, it's alright. I'm just going to call a tow truck," I said, but he already had two feet out the door and was now walking around the front of the car towards me.

"Do you mind if I get into your car?" he asked before getting into the driver's seat.

"Sure," I said moving over and allowing him to get inside the car. He tried starting the car again, but it wouldn't turn over. He got out and walked over to his trunk. He pulled out a yellow box that had two cables attached to it. He hooked it on to the battery and allowed it to sit for a little while. There was an awkward silence and I looked up to him staring at me through his long eyelashes. His eyes were so naturally low that you would think he was either high or asleep. He had this Odell Beckham 'is he or isn't he gay' kind of thing going on. I was praying that he didn't start asking questions that I didn't have a lie for. I pulled out my phone and started walking away from the car then circled back, walking around the car.

"Who's that, ya boyfriend you texting?" John asked.

"I could have sworn I told you, I had no boyfriend. I'm catching Pokémon for Kianni," I said, and he starting laughing.

"Yea, I know. Things change, you never know."

"Whelp, nothing changed over here."

"Good," he said.

"Good, what?"

"Nothing. Alright, get in the car and try to start it," he said. I jumped in the car and turned the key and it started right up.

"Yes, now I can get my butt home. Thank you so much. How can I repay you?"

"You can go to dinner with me," he said, shooting down my whole gay theory.

"No," I answered.

"How about lunch?"

"Not gonna happen. I don't date. I have a son to raise."

"Single moms date," he said trying to convince me to say yes.

"Not me." He put on a sad face like I was disappointing him, but I'm sure he would get over it. He probably had a lot of females throwing themselves at those gorgeous eyelashes and that 6' frame with those muscles ready to bust out of that tight fitting shirt. His perfectly curly Mohawk, those juicy, pink, bubble gum lips, and that chestnut skin complexion. This dude had the potential to do damage to a bitch's mental, and I wasn't trying to be that bitch. This little boy was not about to have me fucked up in the head. He closed the hood of my car and started walking towards me, biting down on his bottom lip. The closer he got, the more his cologne invaded my nostrils, causing my kitty to get frisky. My silly ass did the only thing I could think of. I jumped my ass inside the car before he could see my nipples getting hard and my rings ripping their way through my shirt. I closed up my jacket as he leaned into my window.

"Listen here, Kandice. I'm not the type of guy to take 'no' for an answer when it comes to things I want, and I don't typically want much. The only reason I'm going to let you slide for now is because I know I'll be seeing you again, and I'll have another chance to get you to say yes. So in the meantime, you can repay me by giving me that box of Nerds in your cup holder," he said. I laughed as I lift the armrest and picked out all the Nerds and handed them to him.

"Don't eat them all at once, sweetie. It's almost your bedtime," I said, joking with him.

"You got jokes, alright. We'll see how many jokes you have when I have..." he was saying as he backed away from the car, but I couldn't hear the ending part to his statement.

"What was that?" I asked.

"Nothing, Miss Kandice. You have a good night," he said with a cocky grin on his face, as he jumped into his car and pulled off.

"Damn, that little boy got it going on," I said to myself as I pulled off and out of the parking lot.

John

Wow, so Kandice is Kandi and Kandi is Kandice. I was attracted to the same woman and I had no idea. I wanted to say something, but I didn't want to put her on the spot like that. She was allowed to have a private life and me intruding on that was not going to make my chance of having her any greater. I put two and two together when I looked across the parking lot and recognized her face. Then when she got out of the car, I recognized that body I was just lusting over an hour ago. I would have never taken Kandice to be a stripper, but at the same time, she was a single mother and I know a mother is always going to do what needs to be done for the sake of her child. I felt my phone start to ring.

"Hello," I said answering the phone.

"This is a collect call from an inmate, *Kori*, in Passaic County jail. Press one if you would like to accept," the all too familiar operator said. I shook my head before hitting one.

"John, baby, I need you to come get me from the county," my ex-girlfriend begged on the other end of the phone.

"Again, Kori? What the fuck, man. This the third time this month. I ain't got the money to keep dishing out to bail your ass out," I said, becoming frustrated with this recurring event.

"I know, John, baby. I swear I'll pay you back every penny."

"And how the hell you going to do that, Kori? Yo' ass ain't got no money and when you do get money, you blow that shit away on drugs. I should leave yo' ass up in there. Maybe you'll sober up and get ya fucking mind right."

"Come on, John, please? I'll suck ya dick the way you like it, baby."

"What? Girl, get the fuck off my damn line with that crackhead shit," I said, hanging up the phone. I put the phone in the cup holder and continued to drive. Kori was my ex girl or should I say ex fiancée. Korina and I were together for six years, since high school. I thought she was the one, my future queen, and she was. I proposed to her when we were 21. I expected us to be married by now with a boatload of kids running through the house, but that dream was taken away from me after her third miscarriage. They had run a toxicology screening on her and found large amounts of heroin in her system. I don't know how I could have missed the shit. She was always tired, and she wasn't interested in sex anymore unless she wanted something out of me. Later that night, I searched the obvious places on her body for track marks and came up with nothing. I then went and did some research and checked her again between her fingers and toes, and the bends of her legs; I even found needle marks in her pubic area. I paid for her to get help, but she skipped out on it and went MIA for a month. She showed back up in the county. I got a call from her asking me to come bail her out. When I did go get her, she looked bad. Nothing like the girl I was in love with. She even sold her engagement ring that I dropped over 20 stacks on. I tried numerous times to help her, but you can't help someone who didn't want to be helped. I don't know why it was so hard for me to give up on this girl.

I bust a U-turn on my way, yet again, to bail her out of jail.

Chapter 8

John

It was six in the morning and I stood in the shower allowing the hot water to run over my head. It was Sunday morning and I had to meet my father and brother at my mom's gravesite in an hour. This was an everyday ritual that we did. When my mom was alive, Sundays were her favorite day of the week. Every Sunday she made sure everyone came over at seven in the morning to have breakfast together. When my mom died, we kept that tradition alive by going to visit her and then going to breakfast afterwards. During the spring and summer times, one of us would go pick up breakfast and bring it to the cemetery, and we would sit there and have breakfast with my mother.

As I sat there thinking about the rest of my day, I couldn't keep the thoughts of Kandi out of my mind. That was one beautiful woman and I had to have her. Just thinking about her little performance last night had my dick getting hard, just imagining what she could do in the bedroom. Even the sight of her in that sweat suit was marvelous.

"Damn," I said as I looked down at my hard dick. I grabbed

a hold of it and started to stroke it. Closing my eyes and biting my lip, I imagined Kandice just standing there in that sweat suit she had on last night. That turned me on more than seeing her half naked.

"Shit," I moaned out as I continued to stroke harder and faster until I bust, sending my nut down the shower drain. I leaned against the wall of the shower, exhausted. I finished washing and got out. I walked out the shower and went into my bedroom where I dropped down onto my bed. I looked at the clock and it was 6:35. I still had 20 minutes before I had to meet my brother and father. The cemetery was only five minutes away from me, so I laid there for another ten minutes before getting up to get dressed.

Before leaving the house, I stopped at the guest bedroom to check on Kori. I opened the door and looked inside. The room was empty and bed was still made. I walked over to the bathroom and it was empty in there too. I searched the whole house for Kori and she was nowhere to be found. I decided to take a chance and look downstairs in the basement, which was like my man cave. I went downstairs and I knew exactly what was going on. All of my game systems and my Amazon Fire stick were gone.

"This is what the fuck I get for being nice to a damn junkie," I said out loud. I looked at the time before I shut the lights off and left out to meet my father and brother.

Tech

"Pops, what's going on?" I asked him as I walked up to my mom's headstone and kissed it before giving him a hug.

"Not much, son, just living life, taking it day by day. How about you, son?"

"I'm good, Pops, surviving. You know how I do."

"Yea, I know, I raised you. I just have to make sure. You boys are all I got and if y'all not good, we got a problem," he said. My Pops was so gully at times. I was so lucky to have him as a parent. I honestly don't know where I would be without him, Mom, and John. They were my lifelines, and losing Mom killed a part of me because the three of them were literally all I had.

"Where the hell is your brother?"

"I don't know, Pops. You know that negro is never on time.

It don't matter how long he takes in the mirror and getting dressed, that nigga still gonna be ugly," I said, making my pops laugh as I spread the blanket on the grass and started taking out the platters of food I had picked up from the diner.

"Alright now, that's my boy, he looks just like his daddy."

"So, you ugly too," I said to him. We both laughed.

"What y'all over here he, he and ha, ha-ing about?" John asked, walking over to us and sitting down on the blanket.

"Yo' late, ugly ass, nigga. Now sit down so we can pray and converse with Ma," I said as we all sat down and prayed. When we were done, we started digging in our food.

"What's going on with you, son?" my dad asked John.

"Not much, Pops," he answered.

"Then why you look so bothered?" John took a minute before he answered.

"I bailed Kori out again last night."

"Man, why can't you just say fuck that bitch and move on?" I asked, stuffing some French toast in my mouth. I really

71

didn't like that girl back then when her and my brother were together, and I really can't stand that bitch now. I don't know what it was about that girl, why my brother just couldn't leave her to rot. He was always breaking his neck to help her and she always played him in the end. Yea, she was cute back then, she was the spitting image of Lauren London, but now she just looks like a junkie prostitute whore now.

"It's not that easy, bro. I was with her for six years, so I feel obligated to help her out."

"Nigga, that obligation went out the window when the crackhead sold that 20-thousand-dollar engagement ring for crack."

"Yea, whatever. But I bailed her out and let her stay in my guest bedroom. I woke up this morning and she robbed my ass," he said. I just shook my head.

"That's what yo' ass get, for real. I don't feel the least bit bad for you. What she take?"

"My game systems and my Fire Stick."

"Damn, she got the cave? I should go shoot that bitch. Where the hell I'm gonna go and chill?" I complained. He started giggling. He must've thought I was playing but I really wanted to shoot the hoe now.

"Oh, cut the shit out. You ain't shooting no damn body. Now if he wants to waste his time and money on that girl, that's on him. He has a good heart. Stupid as hell, but he has a good heart," Pops said.

"Yea, whatever. Drop that girl and get with the basketball mom," I said.

"Oh, now you for Kandice? Wasn't you the one saying she was too old for me?" John asked.

"Yea, but old in a good way, like sexy cougar kind of way. She can probably teach you a few things," I said with a smile.

"Son, I think it's best you leave the cougars to ya dad. You just stay in your place, young grasshopper," Pops said.

"Really, Pops, while we sitting here with mom?"

"What? Ya momma was a very understanding woman. She's been gone for too long. She knows her husband has needs, ain't that right, baby girl?" Pops said, patting mom's headstone.

"Oh, you got needs, huh? That's where that hickey on your neck came from, your needs?" John questioned.

73

"What? Pops, you letting them old woman suck on ya neck? You too damn old for that. The only place they need to be sucking is you know where. Oops, sorry, Ma," I apologized, forgetting where we were at for a seconds.

"Aight now, listen. I taught y'all the game. Y'all don't need to worry about your father when it comes to the thang, alright?"

"Pops, what the hell is the thang?" I asked.

"You know, the thang," he said moving his arms and pelvis at the same time like Pops from Wayans *Bros.* when he did the 'bang bang bang' dance.

"That's nasty. Pops, don't ever do that again. Keep that behind closed doors. I'm sure mom is probably turning over in her grave right now," I said. At that moment, the blanket I had laid over my mother's grave started moving.

"What the fuck?" John said, jumping up off the blanket. Pops and I did the same thing.

"See what the hell you done did, Pops? You got momma trying to break out of the grave to come kick yo' ass," I said, as the three of us started backing away from the blanket. The blanket started rising and then it started walking away.

"What the fuck is going on here?" John asked. Pops walked over to the blanket and stepped on the edge of it. A fucking fat ass groundhog came walking from under it.

"Nigga, you ain't see that big ass hole before you laid this damn blanket down?" John asked.

"Hell no, this where we always place the blankets. That shit wasn't there last week," I said.

"Let's pack up and get up out of here for Mom really climb out that hole and beat Pop's ass," John said, causing us to laugh.

"Whatever. Ya momma knew the deal. She knew I ran shit up in that house."

"Yea, ok. So how you explain those black eyes you used to sport when we were younger?"

"I used to run into the cabinets," Pops said.

"Pops, you been living in that house for the past 28 years, how the hell you run into the cabinets that are at least eight feet high?" I asked.

"Look, y'all little niggas just mind ya business and let's get up out of here before that fucking hog come back," Pops said, picking the blanket up off the ground. We all kissed Mom's headstone and left in our separate cars.

******

"Pepper, what the hell yo' crazy ass want? Didn't I tell yo' psycho ass to lose my number?" I yelled into the phone as I continued to drive.

"I know, I'm sorry, baby. I swear I didn't mean it," she begged in the phone.

"What you mean you didn't mean it, heffa? You tried to burn my dick off."

"I knew what I was doing. If you wouldn't have moved, that wouldn't have happened. I've done the Hot Tamale on plenty on people."

"Bitch, you was about to set my god damn dick on fire, what you mean I shouldn't have moved? How would you have liked it if I was hold a fucking torch to ya pussy?"

"We just would have had some fried Catfish," she said, laughing, and making me laugh too.

"Man, get yo' ass off my phone you damn lunatic," I said to

her.

"Oh Tech, stop frontin', you know you feeling the kid. So stop all the chit chat and bring that ass over here so we can finish what we started before you ran like a little bitch."

"No fire?" I questioned.

"Nope, no fire, baby. Just me riding your face all morning," she said. I hung up the phone and made my way back to her house. Pepper was right, I was feeling shawty. She was cute, had a nice body, and was funny as hell. I was able to look past her being a stripper. I mean, shit, a woman gotta do what the fuck she got to do. I respect her hustle. Ma was just crazy as hell.

Chapter 10

John

"Big Mike, my boy, what's good with you?" I asked Mike. He knew I wanted something because I didn't typically call him. It was more of a 'see you when I see you' kind of thing. I needed a favor from him though.

"Same ole same ole, Johnny boy. What do I owe this pleasure?" he asked.

"Kandi, does she work tonight?"

"Ah shit, so you taking my advice, huh?"

"Yea, yea, do she work?" I asked again.

"Yea, she's working tonight. It's a big night and Kandi's the top performer she has to work tonight. She's the moneymaker in this bitch."

"Alright, cool. As long as she's going to be there. Good lookin', Mike," I said, hanging up the phone. I drove to the nearest flower shop where I brought Kandi some roses. I had planned to woo her into a date with me.

Once I had everything I needed for tonight, I was on my

way out the store when my phone started ringing. I took it out my pocket, looking at the screen. *What the hell this nigga want?* I thought.

"Yea," I answered the phone with an attitude.

"Fuck you mean 'yea'?" Cali asked from the other end of the phone.

"Yea, nigga, what the fuck you want, is what I mean."

"Look, whatever. You lucky I need yo' ass, otherwise, I would have cut yo' tongue out ya mouth. Now look, I have an emergency that I need your help with. My client from Virginia was robbed for all his product and he needs a re-up ASAP. I need your men to make a run for me."

"A run when?"

"Like now, is when," he said

"I ain't got the man power right now. There's no trips scheduled for a week, I gave all my drivers the week off. They're off with their families, vacationing and shit. Either you wait until next week or you take that shit yourself," I said.

"Seventy-five grand for you and twenty grand for your men. That's my best offer. I need this done tonight, boy," he said, hanging up on me.

"Who the fuck is he calling boy? I'm gonna kill that nigga one day," I said out loud as I started dialing Tech's number. Ninety grand was too much money to pass up on. I figured I would keep the seventy-five and if Tech agreed to come with me, he could keep the twenty. He did a run with me before and he hated it. I hoped the money would convince him.

"Bro, what's good?" Tech answered the phone. You could hear Fetty Wap's "Jimmy Choo" song playing the background.

"Shit, what you doing?" I asked him.

"I'm over at Pepper's house about to tear that kitty kat up."

"Not until you finish licking it, baby," I heard Pepper say in the background.

"Ewe, you's a nasty motherfucker. Look, you wanna make 20 grand tonight?"

"I want to," Pepper said in the phone.

"Girl, ain't nobody talking to yo' ass. Nigga, take me off speaker."

"My bad, make 20 grand how, bro?" Tech asked.

"That faggot, Cali, asked for a bus to do a run tonight and I gave the guys off this week. You up for a road trip?" I asked.

"Nigga, you know I hate doing them shits. Thirty grand and I'm all yours."

"Twenty-five," I negotiated.

"Fine, what time we leaving?"

"I'll let you know. Let me call this bitch nigga back," I said, hanging up the phone and dialing Cali back.

Kandi

"Kianni, you ready?" I yelled down the hall of my apartment to Kianni's bedroom. I was in the living room lacing up my pink and white retro twelves, about to head to the park and play basketball with Kianni. This was how we spent our mother-son time. At five years old, my son was the king of my world. I would do anything and give anything for him. I was determined to help my son make it out of the ghetto and into the pros. Every now and then, I took him down to the courts and had a one-on-one game with him. For

81

a five-year-old, my son had skills, and with John as his coach, I knew my son was going to be a force to be reckoned with. I remembered hearing about Johnathan during his college years at Seton Hall. He was supposed to get drafted by the NBA but turned it down when his mom died a few years back. There were numerous newspaper articles on him calling him Paterson's next rising star, but I guess things changed. After he graduated, he was hanging around Previous a lot. Like his little junior shadow or something. Johnathan took a special interest in Kianni. He noticed his skills too, and took him under his wing like his little protégé.

I jumped off the coach, because there was a knock at the door. After looking through the peephole, I opened it.

"Hi," I said to the strange man.

"Here you go, I just need you to sign right here," he said, handing me a box.

"I think you have the wrong apartment. It could be Ashley's next door, she's always getting flowers," I said, handing the box back to the delivery man.

"Uh, are you Ms. Kandice?"

"You sure it's not another Kandice in the building?"

"Um, To Kianni's mom, Kandice," he said, reading off the card. I took the box back, signed, thanked the man and shut the door. I opened up the card and read the note.

To Kianni's mom (Kandice), I hope these persuade you to say yes the next time I ask you on a date. I told you I won't stop until you say yes, so until you do, be expecting two dozens of roses delivered to you every single day until you give me the time of day. Stay beautiful,

Johnathan

I closed the card and couldn't erase the smile off my face. *This little boy better cut it out before I rape his little ass,* I thought to myself as I opened the box. I smiled at the sight of the roses. No one has ever sent me flowers like this. I mean, how could they? I blew every man off that tried to talk to me. I was too focused on bettering myself and taking care of my son. Johnathan's little ass on the other hand, didn't know how to take no for an answer. He was persistent. I cleaned out a vase and placed the roses inside before Kianni and I left out.

****

"Come on, Momma, one more game," Kianni called from

the court. I had retired to the bleachers. I was tired as hell. A work out then two games with Kianni was all the exercise I needed.

"I can't, baby, Momma tired. I'm getting old," I said, trying to catch my breath. Kianni came over and sat down next to me.

"You are pretty old, Momma," Kianni said.

"What? Ya momma is not old. I said I'm getting there. I can still beat you in a race. I'm not that old."

"Momma, how come I don't have a dad?" he asked, catching me by surprise. I knew this day was coming but not so soon.

"That's because the man that's supposed to be your dad, had some other things to take care of. He wasn't ready to be a dad and I really wasn't ready to be your mom, but guess what?"

"What?" he asked.

"I got ready. I got ready to be your mom *and* your dad, and that all that matters. You're a special kid because you have both parents in one," I said, trying to make our situation sound better than what it really was.

"Cool," he said sitting back on the bleacher.

"I couldn't have asked for a better son, you know that?" I said, kissing him on the forehead.

"Yea, I know. That's because I'm cool and nice on the court."

"Ewe, you sound so cocky right now. Where did you learn that from?" I asked him.

"Coach John. He said I should be my biggest fan before anyone else. Even you, Momma."

"Well, Coach John is right. He's a smart man. Do you like Coach John?"

"Yes, he's so cool. He has so much money and so many cars, Momma. One day I want to be like him." I continued listening to Kianni boast about Coach John, and I couldn't help but wonder if maybe I should give him a chance. I wasn't a fan of men younger than me, but Johnathan was very mature for his age.

"Come on, let's go to Galotti's and get some ice cream," I said, picking up the basketball and our water bottles. I wanted

85

to get some more mother-son time in before I had to go to work.

Chapter 11

Johnathan

After I was done gassing the bus up, I went and scooped up Tech from his apartment. He came walking out with a suitcase.

"Nigga, you know we only going there to drop off the product and coming back, right?" I said looking at him.

"Yeah, why you ask that?"

"Because you look like you packed for a mini fucking vacation."

"I need shit. I'm about to be on this bus all damn day. Now, can you just mind your business and just drive the shit? Did you get the product yet?" he asked, taking his socks off.

"Not yet. That's where we going now."

"Alright. Afterwards, we have to make a quick stop," Tech said, as he started clipping his toenails in the seat.

"You serious right now with that shit, nigga? When we get back, yo' ass vacuuming this shit. I don't need my customers sitting on ya sharp Jurassic Park toenails."

"Shut up, pussy."

"I got ya pussy," I said, pushing hard on the brakes, which sent Tech's face smacking into the chair in front of him.

"Ah, shit!" he yelled. I was laughing so hard I had to pull over so that I wouldn't crash the bus.

"Fuck you, nigga."

We pulled up to Cali's big ass house that used to be Previous' house. I drove around back and parked the bus near the back door. After beeping the horn twice, the back door came open and three guys came out rolling out brick after brick of cocaine and Venom. I opened up the floors of the bus and allowed them to start loading the product in the floor.

"Gentlemen..." Cali came outside in a silk red robe, one of those bonnet things that the girls be wearing when they don't want to mess up their hair, and the nigga had the nerve to have the Fenti slippers with the fur on the front of them.

"Would you look at the strawberry shortcake pimp," Tech said.

"Don't hate, nigga. I can still pull more pussy than you dressed like this," Cali said.

"Aye, boy, pussy doesn't count. There were rumors going around that you like for the girls to play in your booty hole. It's all good though. I'm all for gay marriage," Tech said, and I couldn't help but laugh. My brother didn't have a filter at all. He wasn't the disrespectful type, but after Cali's punk ass accused us of stealing from him, Tech lost all respect for Cali. He only continued to deal with him because Cali was how I made majority of my money, and Tech knew if I got paid he got paid.

"Keep on talking, black ass. Johnny Boy, here's the address and this is the one and only person you are to release the product to. If you don't see this face, you don't give shit. When you come back, I'll have your money sent to your account," Cali said. I gave him a head nod and continued to wait for his men to be done.

When they were done, Tech and I jumped in the bus and pulled away from the house.

"Where you need to stop? Let's hurry up and get our ass on

89

the road."

"River Drive in Garfield," he said. I followed his direction until we reached our destination. I beeped the horn twice like Tech said.

"What the fuck are we waiting for?" I asked.

"Pepper," he said nonchalantly.

"Nigga, are you fucking stupid? You must be. What the fuck was you thinking inviting that girl with us to do this run? You just met this trick," I seethed.

"Calm down, she won't see nothing go down. We'll just drop her ass off at the mall somewhere while we go make the drop."

"Nigga," I continued at him, but there was a knock at the door of the bus. I walked over and hit the button to let her in. She looked at me and rolled her eyes.

"I got ya trick, nigga," she said, walking to the back of the bus and sitting on Tech's lap.

"Hey, baby," she said followed by a kiss on Tech's lip.

"What's good, baby girl, you ready for a little road trip?"

"Yup," she responded. I put on my seat belt and turned the

bus on.

"Come over here and put ya seat belt on. That nigga up there a little too friendly with the brakes," Tech said, referring to me making him smack his face on the seat in front of him earlier.

****

Five hours later and we were finally arriving in Virginia. We would have been here earlier, but Pepper's ass had to stop and pee like five times on the way down here.

"Where we dropping her off at?" I asked.

"She has a name. You can drop me off at the nearest mall. I have some shopping I need to do," Pepper said. I used the GPS to locate the nearest mall and followed the directions there. I pulled up to the Lynn Haven Mall and opened the door for her to get out.

"Here's my stop," she said, reaching down and giving Tech a kiss on the lips.

"I'll see you in a little bit, baby girl," he said, reaching in his pocket, peeling off a few bills and giving it to her. This chick

91

must've had some good pussy, if she got my brother breaking her off. She stuffed the money in her handbag, walked past me, and mushed me on the side of the head.

"Girl, I don't know where ya hands been," I said.

"In my ass," she said, sticking her tongue out at me. I shut the door and pulled off.

"Don't be treating my boo like that," Tech said from the back seat.

"Next time, you and your boo need to wait until y'all get to a hotel room for that shit," I said to him, letting him know I knew what they were in the back doing. They couldn't have been any more obvious. First they got up and went to the back seat then when I looked in the mirror, I see Pepper's bright ass head moving up and down. I was used to being in the same room as Tech when he was fucking; we used to do it all the time. My parents made us share rooms up until we were 18 and I left for college. We had a sheet we would put up to separate the room whenever one of us would bring a girl over. When he would sneak a chick through the window, I would put my earphones in and turn my music all the way up, and he would do the same thing.

I remember one time I violated the rules. He had brought a

chick over and like always, we put the sheet up, locked the doors, and I put my headphones on. Like 15 minutes into my J-Cole album, the aroma in the room wasn't right. I had to remove my music to make sure I wasn't tripping. I got up out of bed and started sniffing the air. I pulled open the sheets, scaring the both of their asses. That bitch had the whole room smelling like fish. I'm surprised my mother and father ain't smell the shit from down the hall. I opened the window and put that bitch right on out the way she came in. I know Tech had to smell that shit. He was nasty for continuing to fuck the fishy pussy bitch. This nigga had the nerve to say he was going to put her out after he got his nut.

Sitting in the front of the bus, I was praying that bitch's pussy was fresh because if not, I was putting her ass out on the side of the road. One thing I hated was a bitch whose hygiene wasn't a top priority. Never trust a bitch with fishy coochie.

"Man, shut up. Wake me up when we get there," Tech said.

"I hope the pussy was worth those bills you just gave shorty," I said.

"Shiiit, it was worth more than what I just broke her off. I might just buy that bitch a car when we get back to Jersey," Tech said, laying the seat back and wrapping the blanket around him. I shook my head at him and continued to follow the GPS to the location.

It took about 15 minutes for us to get where we needed. I call the number Cali had written down on the paper; no one answered. As I was about to call again, a text came through from the number telling me to pull around to the garage and back the bus in. I followed the directions. I checked my gun and made sure the shit was loaded. I didn't trust no nigga if it wasn't my brother.

"Yo," I called to Tech, but he didn't wake up. I picked up one of my Nike flip flops and threw it at him.

"What?" he jumped up.

"We're here, Sleeping Beauty. You strapped?" I asked him.

"When am I ever not strapped?" he responded, coming up to the front seat and checking out the surroundings. We had never been here before, so we had to stay alert and watch everything that moved. But the funny thing was that, nothing or no one was moving. You know how they say the quiet before the storm? Well that's exactly what I felt like this was. They left us sitting in this bus waiting for too long. This shit ain't feel right at all.

"Bro, I ain't feeling this shit at all," Tech said, reading my mind.

"I was just thinking the same shit. You think we should pull up out of here?" I asked him.

"Hell yea, with the muthafuckin' quickness," Tech said, sitting back in the seat. I reached over and placed my seat belt back on and was about to turn the bus on, when someone tapped on the door. I looked over at my brother before I pushed the handle to open the door to the bus.

"Where the product?" some big Debo ass nigga asked.

"Nigga, where the dough?" Tech asked, getting up out his seat. Him and Debo had a stare off for what felt like minutes. When the Debo dude realized Tech wasn't backing off, big dude whistled and another came running towards the bus with a duffle bag. Debo took the bag from his guy and pushed it in Tech's chest hard, sending Tech falling into the seat. I knew it was time for me to intervene when Tech started reaching towards his waistband.

I attempted to jump up from my seat but I forgot I had put my seat belt on, so I was unable to reach Tech in time to stop him. Tech pulled out his piece and placed it dead center of Debo's forehead. A bunch of Debo men came running up to the bus with guns. *How the fuck did they know what was going on, I'll never know.*

"T, man, just put the gun down and give the man the product so we can get the fuck up outta here alive," I said to him. He thought about it and then slowly started to lower his gun.

"You muthafuckers better realize who y'all fucking with. I'll shoot his big ass in the face quick. Have my brother drive this bitch right over ya little mans and all them out there," Tech said, but he wasn't putting no fear in big man's heart. Big man just straight smiled in my brother's face and walked around him towards the opening of the floor. He pulled out one of the bricks and a pocket knife. He pushed the knife in the brick and pulled back out and licked it.

"That's not icing, fat motherfucker," Tech said making me chuckle, because he really did just molest that knife with his tongue.

"Nah, this shit ain't right," Debo said, reaching into the floor and pulling another brick out. He did the same with the knife and the molestation. I turned my head for a quick second.

Poof, I heard come from the back of the bus causing me to turn around. Tech was covered in white powder. He looked like the Pillsbury Dough Man. I wanted to laugh but now wasn't the time.

"Y'all niggas trying to play me, bringing me some bullshit. What the fuck boss supposed to do with flour, open up a bread shop?" Debo asked, walking closer to Tech who was still standing there stunned and covered in flour.

"Look, man, we ain't got shit to do with this shit, we just make the drop offs," I said, trying to calm big man down.

"I don't give a fuck," he was saying, when Tech pulled his burner back and placed a bullet in between his eyes. His body fell on top of Tech, which caused him to fall in the seat behind him.

"Oh shit." I quickly sprung into action as I jumped in the driver's seat and quickly shut the door before the niggas in front of the bus could get in. I turned the bus on and pushed down on the gas and drove up out of there.

97

"Yo, toss that bag out the window," I said to Tech, referring to the bag of money. I ain't need this shit on my hands.

"Fuck that, I'm taking my cut out this bitch because I'm bodying Cali's ass as soon as we get back to the town. Nigga set us up big fucking time, man," Tech said, going through the bag and taking stacks out. I couldn't argue with him. When I looked back in the mirror, Tech's ass was still taking stacks out the bag.

"Nigga, throw the fucking bag out the window," I said. I was almost out the gate and I wanted to leave that bag here. I wasn't about to get caught up in a drug deal gone wrong. If they were going to be after anybody, it was going to be Cali's pussy ass.

"What the fuck we gone do with this nigga?" Tech asked about Debo's dead body. I drove down the highway trying to get as far away as possible from that house and at the same time, trying to find somewhere to dump the body. I pulled over on the side of the highway next to the cement divider that was there, to block cars from going over and into the river. I pulled over close enough so that no one could see what we were doing. I got out the driver's seat and helped Tech roll the body over towards the door.

"How the fuck we getting this big nigga over this fucking

wall?" Tech asked.

"We about to lift his ass. On my count," I said counting to three, and we both lifted Debo up and dropped him over and into the river. I shut the door and sat back in my seat.

"This shit is yo' fault, nigga. You got me into this shit, dawg. I should have just said no when you asked me to take this ride with you. But I'm happy I was here because yo' ass would probably be dead right about now," Tech said, taking off his flour and blood covered shirt and pants. He reached into his bag and pulled out a new outfit.

"This is why I come with a bag. I be needing shit," Tech said, getting dressed.

"Man, imagine if I had sent Ben and King out here. They asses would probably be dead because of me. I'm terminating that fucking contract with Cali. He gotta find someone else to run his shit. I can't be putting niggas' lives in jeopardy fucking with Cali."

The bus got quiet. Tech had laid his head back on the headrest and I was lost in my thoughts as I drove down the highway, until Tech's phone started to ringing.

"Oh shit," he said as he answered his phone.

"We right down the street, baby girl," he continued, and that's when I remembered the stripper.

I got off at the next exit to make a U-turn. I had completely forgotten about her. That would have been some fucked up shit if we had left her down here.

Ten minutes later, we were pulling up to the mall.

"I'm about to run to the bathroom. She said she would be by the food court, so I'll go find her," Tech said, getting off the bus. I sat there going through my phone. I pulled up Kandice's number and thought about sending her a text, but that was some creep shit. She never gave me her number; I got it off Kianni's basketball paperwork. It was now five in the afternoon. I figured we would be back in Jersey by nine and I would still be able to make it to the club to see Kandice's performance. I knew she got the flowers I sent to her by now.

I got off the bus, because I needed to stretch my legs. My ass was starting to hurt from sitting in this seat all this time. As I was going through my phone, a text message came through from Cali asking *where the fuck we were.* He probably got the phone call about the deal gone bad, but I ain't give a shit. He had an ass whooping coming his way. I was sending all his calls and text messages to my block list. I wanted to talk to him face-to-face.

I was on the side of the bus when I felt something hard pressing against the back of my head.

"Hands up, motherfucker," this person said. I shook my head. *Did I really just get caught slipping?*

"Turn around," he said and I did as he asked.

"You really about to do this in front of the mall and all these cameras?"

"Shut the fuck up," he said, taking out his phone. I looked behind him and couldn't stop myself from laughing at the way Pepper crouched down and was sneaking up behind him.

"The fuck so funny?" he asked.

"Nothing, man," I answered just as Pepper swung the fifty bags she had in her hand at the guy's head, causing the guy to stumble. I followed up with a left hook to the face, sending him to the ground.

"Get on the bus, Pepper," I yelled to her.

"Wait, my shoes," she said, picking up her bags. I ran up on dude, kicked the gun out his hand, and started stomping him. He grabbed on to my foot, causing me to fall to the ground. The guy attempted to get up and go for the gun, but I grabbed his foot and twisted it. I knew for sure I broke this nigga's ankle. I got up to get at him some more, and dude used his good foot to kick my ass in the side of the head. I don't know how I forgot this nigga had another foot. He was able to get to the gun just as I gained my senses back, and I jumped on top of him just as he picked the gun up. I grabbed the gun and we were now both on the ground fighting for possession of it when the gun went off. I heard someone moaning behind me but was too preoccupied to see who. I let one of my hands go and was now sitting on top of him, punching him with my free arm.

"What the fuck?" I recognized Tech's voice. He came up and started helping me with dude, stomping him all in his shit, until he laid there with little fight left in him. I was able to gain full control and I stood above him with the gun in my hand. I heard someone moaning from behind me. I turned and Pepper was laid up against the bus holding on to her shoulder. Her hand was covered in blood. Tech and I both ran up to her.

"Get her in the bus," I told him as he scooped her up and was bringing her onto the bus.

"I know y'all niggas ain't about to leave my shoes. Go get them," she demanded. If she ain't just damn near save my life I wouldn't have gotten shit. I picked up her bags and got on the bus. I got Pepper to the nearest hospital to get her arm taken care of. I had to give it to the stripper though. She took that gunshot like a G. I really did owe shawty for helping a nigga out. Another chick would have probably said to hell with that shit and ran in the other direction. She earned my respect today.

By the time we got back to Jersey and dropped Pepper off home, it was about eleven o'clock. Cali was blowing my phone up but I was curving that nigga like a bitch. I went home, showered, got dressed, and was back out the door on my way to Velour.

Chapter 12

Kandi

I was in my dressing room, struggling to put in these contacts I had decided to wear for my performance tonight. June was having a Platinum theme party for some new rap artist who had just gotten signed to a major record label. I wanted to turn this performance down, but there was a special request for me to perform tonight. I didn't see what was so special about my performances that everyone loved. I ain't gon' lie, I was the shit, but that was only because I was older and knew that less is more. I didn't need to flip upside down or surfboard another bitch down a pole. All I did was step on stage and make every man in the room feel as if I was dancing for him and him only. Every man wants a lady in the street and a freak in the sheets, so I made my performance gracefully sophisticated, wearing next to nothing. That alone made niggas empty out their bank accounts, their wives' bank accounts, joint bank accounts, and their kid's piggy banks. I wasn't sure how much longer I was going to do this, I just knew it wasn't for much longer.

I was so in my zone I had completely forgotten I wasn't in the dressing room alone, until I heard one of the other girls say Pepper had gotten shot today.

"What? Where was she shot, is she ok?" I asked Charlie, the naïve white girl who wanted to be everyone's friend.

"She speaks," Charlie said, trying to be funny. I gave her a look and she continued.

"Yea, she's ok. She was just shot in the shoulder, she'll be good."

"Good to know," I said, turning back around. I heard someone suck their teeth.

"Bitches wanna act like they care and shit. Fuck outta here," Keisha said. Keisha was Pepper's best friend and one of the biggest hoes in this place. Her and Pepper were the ones tricking in the back rooms. I was able to deal with Pepper, but I couldn't stand this bitch, Keisha.

"Excuse me? And who exactly is the recipient to that little comment you just made?" I asked, turning back around to face Keisha.

"You, grandma. You ain't never give a shit about her before. Don't act like you do now."

"Bitch, who the fuck you calling grandma?" I jumped up out of my seat, going after Keisha's throat.

"Oh, not tonight ladies," Big Mike said, coming in the room just in time. Charlie must've known it was about to go down and she ran out and got Mike.

"Come on, sis, she don't want it," Mike said, sitting me back down in my chair.

"I'm gone ring that bitch's neck one day, I promise you, Mikey. And you better not stop me or I'm hooking off on you after."

"I know. Don't worry about that bitch. It's money to be made out there and you don't need to be getting all ugly and sweaty if it ain't for making that dough."

"Word," I said, picking up my lip plumper. I paid all that

money for lipo in a bottle and it was well worth it, because they had my lips nice and thick like I always wanted them.

"How's Rosanne doing?" I asked him about his wife.

"Roxy is good. Kids still driving her crazy. I asked June's ass for some time off so that I could give her a break from the kids, and this nigga had the nerve to say no. I promise you the minute I find another gig, I'm off this shit," Mike said.

"I don't blame you. June is a fucking dick."

"That's your baby daddy," he said low.

"Involuntarily, but I love that little boy to death. So let's get off that subject. Y'all ever thought about signing them up for sports? Kevin is eight, he can play basketball with Kianni, and Darla is six, she can be on the cheerleading squad. That'll give Roxy a little time to herself. During practice, she can drop them off and go. If she wants, some days I can pick them up and drop them off for her," I said, double checking my perfect face. He started cracking up laughing about something.

"What's so funny?" I asked.

"You know damn well Darla ain't putting no cheerleading

skirt, on and damn damn well Kev ass ain't playing with no basketball. I can guarantee any amount of money, Kevin wants to do cheerleading and Darla is going to want to play ball," he said, shaking his lowered head. Then I started laughing. I forgot his kids had that role reversal thing going on.

I noticed that during Darla's birthday party, Kevin was more interested in the makeup and fairy princess stuff, and Darla couldn't care less. His son wanted to be a girl and his daughter wanted to be a boy. It was something severely screwed up with his sperm cells. He was always blaming it on Roxy's eggs, but the gender is determined through the male's sperm.

"Oh yea, my bad. Either way, it's 2016, no one would even bat an eye," I said.

"Don't be laughing at my family, nugget head. That actually sounds like a great idea though. I'll see what's up with that," he said, looking at his watch. The dressing room door opened again.

"Oh, here's where the party's at?" June asked coming through the door. I rolled my eyes so hard I think I saw my damn brain.

"Don't you have a job to do?" he said to Mike. Mike looked

at me and rolled his eyes.

"I'll see you out there, sis," Mike said, standing up to leave. As he walked past June, June looked him up and down like the bitch that he was. I don't think his issue was with Mike not working. It was the fact that Mike was sitting next to me.

I looked at myself in the mirror, making sure I was perfect, and I was. I looked like a sexy ass platinum doll, in my cute little two-piece outfit, my hair in a high ponytail that hung all the way down to my butt, and my makeup was gorgeous although it was about to be hidden behind a mask. June sat there staring at me with lust in his eyes. I ignored him, grabbed my mask and was about to walk past him, when he grabbed my wrist.

"Meet me in my office later on tonight," he whispered in my ear.

"You must be out ya mind," I said, snatching my arm away from him. I noticed all the other girls looking. I left his ass standing there as I walked straight out the door.

"Fuck y'all looking at?" I heard him ask before the door shut behind me.

Johnathan

I sat in the back of the club in the cut, watching the performances. Some of these girls were actually aight, but they didn't have anything on Kandi. I ordered me a Red Bull and a double shot of Henny so that I wouldn't fall asleep. I was tired as shit, but I was determined to see Kandi. I don't know how big Mike spotted me, but he started walking over to me.

"What's up, John, what you doing here?" he asked with a smirk on his face.

"Shut yo' ass up, nigga. You know why I'm here."

"Yea, I know, I was just messing with you. Yo' ass look like you about to pass the fuck out," Mike said.

"Yea, I'm fucking tired, man. But I have a mission to accomplish," I said.

"You know me and her pretty cool. That's like sis right there. I can always put in a good word for you,"

"Nah, I got this, but thanks anyway. You know whenever you ready to leave this bitch, I can always use more drivers. I'll help you get your CDLs and everything."

"Alright, that sounds pretty good. I just need to know what you paying, but I'll holla at you about that tomorrow. I'm about to go post up. She's up next, by the way," Mike said, walking away, just as the lights dimmed like last time, and candy started falling from the sky again. I sat up at full attention just like every other nigga in this bitch. The spotlights turned on and the hook to Lil Wayne's "She Will" song came on.

Uh, she just started to pop it for a nigga

And look back and told me "baby, it's real"

And I say I ain't doubt you for a second

I squeeze it and I can tell how it feel

I wish we could take off and go anywhere but here baby you know the deal

But she bad, so maybe she won't

Uh, but shit then again maybe she will."

Just like last time, she had me on the edge of my seat with the way she moved her body so sensually to the rap music. I

111

had never seen anyone twerk with grace. One minute into the song, it switched to Kelly Rowland's song "ICE". This really sent me overboard because Kelly was my celebrity crush next to Tika Sumpter and Gabrielle Union. What can I say? I really had a thing for chocolate.

You're like ice
I-C-E,
Feels so nice, scorching me,
You're so hot hot
Baby, your love is so hot, hot
Pull up,
She been purring like a kitten
Cravin' your love
I've been counting down the days you been gone
A little too long, patient
Knowing exactly what it is
It lasts time and now

By now, I was out of my seat and standing up, as she rolled over from her back onto all fours and put an arch in her back that looked like it hurt, but it was sexy as hell. It reminded me of bunny ears, the way her ass looked pointed up in the air like that.

"Fuck," I unintentionally said out loud. I really felt like I had no control of my body as I watched the rest of her performance. By the time she was finished, I couldn't leave like I wanted to. My legs were so numb that I just collapsed onto the couch. Once I was able to gain control of my body, I left out the club and jumped in my car, in search of her car. When I found it, I parked next to it got out and went straight to my trunk. I took the boxes of roses out and placed the four dozen of roses on the hood of her car. I opened the other box of rose petals and started spelling out "Go Out With Me" in front of her car. I had gotten some of the electronic candles and placed them in between the letters. When I was done, I got back in my car and waited for her to come out.

I was out there for a minute; it was now 2:30. I know the club closed at two so I didn't mind waiting a little longer. I texted Mike and asked if he was still inside, but he had left already. I got out my car and walked around to the front of the club. The front parking lot was empty.

"Where the hell is she?" I said to myself as I turned to walk back to my car. I heard the front door of the club bust open, causing me to turn around. It was Kandice who had bust through the door and was now getting up from the ground. I ran over to her.

"Kandice, you alright?" I asked her. She was crying, out of breath, and she had blood on her shirt.

"John, what are you doing here?" she asked.

"I asked you a question first, Kandice. Why are you crying? What happened to you?" I asked again. She wiped her face.

"Fucking June's ass just tried to rape me," she said.

"Where is he, Kandice?" I asked, pulling out my gun. She turned and looked at me and then my gun.

"Hopefully in his office dying from blood loss," she said. I grabbed her hand and brought her back into the club with me.

"Where's his office?"

She led me to his office where I could hear him moaning. I pushed her behind me and I opened the already cracked door. He was sitting on the ground with his pants around his ankle, bleeding from an ink pen stuck inside his ribcage.

"Ah shit, help me, man. That crazy bitch stabbed me," he said.

"Fuck you calling a bitch?" Kandice said, running from behind me and kicking him in the face. I couldn't help but laugh. Shawty was mad gangsta. I was loving it.

"You stupid bitch. I'm gonna kick yo' ass, you just wait and see. And your ass is fired, you dumb bitch."

"You got one more time to call her a bitch and then you and I are gonna have a problem. Don't be the second nigga I dump in the river today," I said to the asshole on the floor.

"Kandice, what you wanna do with him?"

"Just leave his skanky ass on the floor. I got a better way to ruin his life," she said, picking up her purse and placing her items that were scattered all over the floor inside, and then walking out of the office. I put my gun back in my waistband and followed behind her.

Kandi

I couldn't believe my luck today. This was probably one of the worst nights of my life next to me getting pregnant by June. John was following me as I quickly walked out the club. I was so embarrassed that he caught me in this predicament, but glad that he was here at the same time.

"Kandice, wait up," he said, walking behind me. I ignored him and kept on walking.

"Kandice," he called again.

"What, John?"

"Will you wait? I need to know that you're ok," he said.

"I'm fine," I said, wiping at the tear that fell from my eye.

"No you not, wait up," he said, grabbing my arm, stopping my fast pace. I turned around and faced him. He just stared in my eyes for a minute. He was such a gorgeous man. I didn't see what it was about me that he liked. Why wasn't he in the face of one of these younger chicks running around here?

"You're not fine, Kandice. What can I do to help you?" he asked.

"There's nothing you can do. I just want to get home and get in the bed with my baby," I said.

"Did you get my flowers?" he asked. I smiled at the thought of the roses sitting home on my kitchen counter.

"Yes, I did. How did you know where I live?"

"Research," he said. I looked at him.

"You mean stalking?" I asked and he laughed.

"You can say that, but I only stalk beautiful woman that I like, who play hard to get."

"No one is playing hard to get. I'm just not trying to focus on anything else that ain't about me or my kid. I have to get myself straight before I can focus on a man."

"So don't focus on me, Ma. I'm straight. let me focus on you. Let me wine and dine and spoil you. I can tell a woman who deserves the world just by looking. All I want to do is take you out, show you I'm nothing like these other niggas out here. I'm 25 with the mind focus of a grown ass man. I have my own business, my own house, cars, never been arrested— or should I say never been caught—I'm educated, cute, and got good hair," he said, making me laugh.

"Good, hair, yea. Cute? I'm not too sure about cute."

"So are you going to let me take you out?" he asked.

"What are you doing here anyway?" I asked him.

"I was enjoying the show. What you doing here?" he asked.

"Typically, I would have lied, but I know you heard him say I was fired."

"Yea, I did," he said smiling, and pulling out a box of strawberry Nerds and started pouring some in his mouth.

"You knew that though. You just wanna be a jerk, huh?"

"I know; I just don't like assuming things out loud. Want some, Kandi?" he asked, holding out the box of Nerds.

"Yup," I said, snatching the box out his hand and turning to walk to my car. When I turned the corner and got closer to my car. I was a little confused by what was going on.

"Yea, it's been out here for a while. It said go out with me, but you didn't come out in time, so the wind messed my shit up," he said. I turned around to him.

"You did this for me?"

"Yea, and me also. I really like you, Kandice, but you be playing a nigga out." I turned back around and walked over to my car, and picked up the four bundles of roses as a smile spread across my face.

"Ok," I said.

"Ok, you'll let me take you out?"

"Yes, you can take me out."

"Ok, come on," he said, catching me off guard.

"Come on where?"

"I'm taking you out," he said, grabbing my hand.

"I meant like another day," I replied.

"Nope. I'm not sending you home to think about it and you change ya mind. Get in the car," he stated clicking the alarm. I stood there.

"I have a son that I have to get home to."

"Who's with him now?"

"I have a sitter."

"Ok. Well, call ya sitter and give me the phone," he said.

"No, why?"

"Girl, just call the sitter and pass me the phone," he said. That demanding shit was secretly turning me on. I took out my phone and called Saniyah, my babysitter. She was probably sleeping too, but I figured I would give it a try. She was a sweet 16-year-old girl. She was looking to make some money so she had posted fliers for babysitting jobs, and thankfully, I got to her first before anyone else. I had a sit down with her mom because the hours I needed were overnight. I needed confirmation from her mom first that the hours were okay before I hired her. Her mom said it was okay as long as she could come and take a look around my place, to make sure it was a safe environment for her kid to be. I didn't blame her. This was a crazy world and I would have done the exact same thing. Since she's been working for me, me and her mom had become cool. All of a sudden, I started feeling bad because with June firing me, I wasn't going to need Saniyah anymore until I found another job.

"Hello," she answered sleepily.

"Hey, Saniyah, hun. Sorry I woke you," I apologized.

It's ok, Ms. Kandice. Are you stuck at work again?" she asked.

"Um, no, not really, sweetie. I have someone that wants to talk to you and no matter what he says, you can always say no, ok?" I said, trying to coach her over the phone to say 'no'. John took the phone from me and put it on speaker.

"Hey, Saniyah, my name is John. I'm Kianni's basketball

coach."

"The one who brought Ms. Kandice the roses?" He looked at me and smiled.

"Yup, that's me. Ms. Kandice has any other flowers there?" he asked.

"Excuse you, nosey," I said.

"No, just those."

"Good. If Ms. Kandice gets any flowers from anyone else except me, throw them in the garbage," he said, making Saniyah laugh and me as well.

"Look, I need a favor. I need you to stay with Kianni a little while longer, maybe until about noon. I wanna take Ms. Kandice on a date. I'll give you an extra fifty dollars," he said.

"Make it a hundred and I'll stay until one," she said, bargaining. I laughed. Saniyah was about her money and I didn't blame her.

"Alright, you got it, little lady."

"Cool, now can I go back to sleep?"

"Yup, have a good night," he said handing me back my phone.

"Alright, Saniyah, I'll see you in a few. Kiss Kianni for me," I said before hanging up the phone.

"Get in the car," he said, now standing there with the car door open for me to get in.

"You're kind of bossy, you know that? The magic word is please, you ain't learn that from Barney?" I said as I got in the car.

"Who's Barney?" he inquired. I looked at him like he was crazy.

"You better be shitting me?"

"I am, put your seat belt on," he replied as we pulled off.

****

I'm not sure how long I was in the car for, because I had fell asleep, but I was awakened by something tickling my nose. I opened my eyes to John blowing my hair in front of my face with his breath.

"Ewe, ya breath smell like a stripper pole," I said, rubbing my eyes. He started laughing.

"Whatever. My breath smells good, hater," he said, showing me the gum he had in his mouth.

"Give me a piece," I said with my hand out.

"The magic word is please, you ain't learn that from Barney?" he said, flashing that August Alsina smile with them bright white teeth.

"Please, can I have some gum?"

"Huh," he said, holding the gum he was chewing on his tongue. He must ain't know who he was dealing with. I reached over and with my mouth, I took his gum right out his mouth, sat back in my chair and started chewing it. I pulled the mirror down and started fixing my hair, as he sat there stunned that I had just done that.

"You nasty," he said.

"I'm a stripper. Where are we?" I asked, reaching in my bag for my brush to fix my wild and curly hair.

"AC," he said. I pushed the mirror up and started looking around.

"I was not sleep that long."

"Yea you were. Snoring and all, baby girl. You sleep hard for someone with a kid."

"Yea, but no matter how hard I sleep, I can hear a baby cry from a mile away. That's a special power moms have. You ever waited for the door to shut and start talking shit about ya mother and she yell back, 'I heard that'?"

"Hell yea, all the time."

"Special mom powers."

"Come on, get out," he said, opening his door and getting out. I closed up my lip gloss and got out. I walked around to the trunk where he was. He had a bunch of bags inside. He went inside one of them and pulled out a T-shirt.

"Here. I picked this up for you, so you could change out that bloody shirt," he said, handing me the shirt.

"When did you get this?"

"Like I said, you sleep hard, Ma. Slob and everything."

"You's a lie, she doesn't slob," I said, taking the shirt from him.

"I don't know who *she* is, but *you* was drooling like a

teething baby," he said.

"Shut up, you so dumb," I said as I removed my shirt, standing in nothing but my lace bra. I quickly placed the other shirt over my head. I noticed him looking around and then he looked at me.

"Just like that, huh?" he said.

"I'm a stripper. This is a nice shirt, thank you."

He reached in the trunk and grabbed some other bags and a blanket, and closed the trunk.

"Come on," he said, grabbing my hand as we walked out of the parking garage and on to the boardwalk. We really were in AC. I really can't believe I slept that long. The boardwalk was empty which was to be expected. It was going on six in the morning. We got to the edge of the boardwalk and he stopped me in my tracks, then bent down and started untying my sneakers. He removed them both and then did his own. We continued walking on to the sand. We walked until he found a spot and laid the blanket out on the sand.

"Sit," he said.

"Yes, boss man," I said, sitting down on the blanket. I looked out into the ocean and watched the waves. The cool breeze from the waves felt great on my face. The sun was just starting to rise in the sky and the only sound you could hear was the crashing waves and the seagulls, fighting and scavenging for food. John sat down next to me and started unpacking the bags. He had picked up some breakfast on the way down here while I was sleep. I can't believe I really slept through all of that.

"I wasn't sure what you preferred, so I got a little bit of everything," he said opening up platters of food.

"Damn, you sure did get a bit of everything. I hope you don't think I'm going to eat all this food," I said, referring to the eggs, bacon, sausage, home fries, pancakes, waffles, biscuits, grits, and the fruit salad.

"No, I don't. I know you gotta keep that figure up," he said, placing a plate in front of me and then himself.

"What would you like?" he asked.

"A little bit of everything," I said. I was hungry, so I was ready to go in. He made my plate and then he made his own. We sat eating, talking, and getting to know each other. The more I learned about him, the more I was starting to like him.

"How old do you think I am?" I asked him.

"That doesn't matter to me. Age ain't nothing but a number," he answered.

"Ok, but how old do you think I am?" I asked. He put his fork down and looked at me.

"Early thirties," he said.

"Do I look like I'm thirty?" I asked him.

"No, you look about twenty-five, but you act like a woman of much more life experience and maturity. How old are you, really? If you don't mind me asking," he said.

"I'll be thirty, next week," I said, reaching into the platter for another piece of bacon.

"She's a Leo," he said.

"Damn right, best sign ever," I said like the proud Leo I was.

"Fuck out of here. Aries are the best. We the leaders of the pack."

"Whatever," I replied, lying back on the blanket. "What time is it?"

"A quarter to seven. Why, you got somewhere to be?"

"Yea, sleep," I said, closing my eyes.

"Yo ass got the itis now," he joked.

"Shut up. Come lay down with me," I said, waving him over. He closed all the platters and moved them off the blanket. He laid down on his side and stared at me.

"You have an eye problem? You always staring," I asked.

"Yes, I do stare at you a lot. You're beautiful, Kandice. What man wouldn't want to stare at you? You have an alluring aura to you, it's like innocence. You can probably assassinate the president and I still wouldn't see no wrong in your actions," he said. His words made me smile. No one has ever spoken to me the way he did. Then again, I didn't let anyone else get close enough to me to speak words. I have been abstinent from sex since June got me pregnant. Since then, it's been all about Kianni. I barely got aroused by a man until the night John helped me with my car.

"You trying to get some booty, aren't you?" I asked him and he started laughing.

"Girl, get out of here. I don't want no stripper booty," he said, this time making me laugh.

"Fuck is stripper booty?" I asked him.

"That right there," he said, pointing at my booty.

"Whatever. I'm sure you'll jump at the chance to get some of this stripper booty."

"You damn right. I'll break my neck," he said, looking up in the sky. I sat up and rolled on top of his 6'3, 200-pound muscular body. He wrapped one of his arms around my waist and kept the other one behind his head, as I reached down and kissed him on the lips.

"What was that for?" he asked.

"Ya lips looked good," I said.

"Oh yea? Well how did they taste?"

"They were aight. Kinda taste like hotdog water," I said.

"You bugging, girl, my shits are good," he said, rolling over on top of me, opening my legs so he could lay in between them.

129

"You know something; ya lips looked like they taste good too. Like strawberry Starburst," he said.

"Probably not. I got pork breath right now from them sausages," I said, expecting him to do the same thing I did by kissing my lips.

"I wasn't talking about those lips, hun," he said, catching me off guard, at the same causing my kitty to get frisky.

"Wow, you are a perv. How many of my performances have you seen?"

"Two," he replied, reaching down and pressing his lips against mine. Our tongues somehow found their way to each other because next thing I know, we were tonguing each other down. He grabbed a hold of my waist and adjusted me under him. I don't know why; I've always been weird, but I loved when a man gripped me by my waist.

"Strawberry Starburst," he said, now kissing me on my neck.

"I thought you weren't talking about those lips."

"I wasn't."

"Well, there's only one way to find out," I said, looking up at him, and he smiled down at me with a devilish grin.

"I guess so," he said, moving his head down to waistline.

Was this really about to happen right here on the beach? No, he's not serious, I thought to myself as his fingers started lining the waistband of my tights and they slowly started to ease their way down. Thank God I always washed after a performance.

Johnathan

I wasn't the type of nigga to eat a chick out on the first time, but I'd been dying for a piece of Kandi and I wasn't about to pass up this chance. She must've thought that I wasn't going to do it, but I was serious when I said I wanted to taste those lips. I slid her tights down, revealing the sexy, baby blue thong she had on. The crazy thing is that baby blue was my favorite color. I looked up at her and she covered her face. I smiled and continued to bite down on the thong, moving it to the side. I couldn't strip her down like I wanted to, but this right here was good enough for me. She removed her hands from her face and looked down at me as I went to work, never breaking eye contact. I was hooked after the first lick. I couldn't get enough. So much so that I forgot we were outside in public for a minute. I licked and sucked on her clit until my jaws started getting tired, but I ain't stopped. Especially after she grabbed my head. I started digging her shit out with my tongue and I was right. This shit tasted like rainbows, unicorns, and sprinkles. Don't ask me what the hell that shit tasted like, but it was amazing. Magically fucking delicious. I felt her body start to shake and her moaning became louder. I knew it was over. A half of minute later, she laid there motionless and out of breath. I placed a soft kiss on my new friend and put her panties back where I got them from. I pulled up her pants came back up to her eye level. I reached down and kissed her on her beautiful lips.

"You got a little something right there," she said, pointing to my top lip.

"I know, I was saving some for later," I said.

"So was it strawberry Starbursts to you?" she asked. I wanted to say hell motherfucking yea.

"Nah, more like the yellow Starbursts," I said and she laughed.

"Oh hell no. What you tryna say? I got mediocre coochie?" I laughed at her. She was funny as hell. I like that she was able to go back to back with me with the jokes. I appreciated a woman that could make my serious ass laugh.

"Nah, I'm joking, baby. I could eat you all day long, just in a more private space."

"What time is it?" she asked.

"Going on nine. You wanna go do some gambling?" I asked her.

"I would like to lay here and go to sleep, but we can go do a little gambling. I got some dollars to spare at the slots," she said, sitting up.

"Let's go then," I stated, helping her up from the floor. I picked up the blanket and the food. I threw the food in the garbage and left the blanket sitting on the bench. We went into Tropicana; she wanted to play the slots. She insisted on using her money, but I wasn't having that. She worked hard for her money and I wasn't about to have her blowing that shit on slots. I told her she was wasting her time on these slots, and that the table was where the money was at. She finally gave in and let me open her up to Blackjack and the Roulette table. Once she got the hang of it, I left her alone and I went over to the poker table.

An hour in and my phone started going off. I took it out my pocket and it was Tech.

"Bro, what's going on?" I answered the phone.

"That bitch nigga, Cali, put word out that he's looking for you."

"So, that nigga can suck my dick, put that word out."

"Say the word, me and Dre will go pop that nigga's shit off his shoulder."

"Nah, I'll handle that nigga when I get back in town."

"Back in town? Where the hell yo' ass at?" he asked.

"AC, nigga. We about to be on our way back now," I said.

"We? Who the fuck is we?"

"You so damn nosey. None of your damn business. I'll see you when I get back," I said, hanging up the phone. I checked out the game and went back over to Kandice. Before I could get to her, she came running up to me dancing.

"I won eight hundred dollars," she said, dancing.

"Alright, alright now, turn down, we ain't at the club."

"Bands'll make her dance, bands'll make her dance," she continued dancing. I'm sure she made three times that at the club. I think it was the fact that she won that had her so excited.

"Congratulations. Come on, let's go cash you out so we can get up out of here," I said, wrapping my arm around her and leading her to the cashier's desk.

Chapter 13

Kandi

"Yes, home sweet home," I said, seeing the Paterson signs as we got off the parkway and on to Highway 80.

"Damn, our date was that bad that you ready to leave me already?" John asked.

"I'm ready to kiss my baby boy, take him to practice, and go take a nap," I said.

"Can I come take a nap with you?" he asked, pulling out his ringing phone.

"Uh, you have a basketball team to go coach, so there won't be no napping for you."

"That's what assistant coaches are for. Hold on, baby girl. Bro, I told you I'll deal with Cali's ass later. That pussy don't put fear in my heart," he said into his phone.

Hearing the name Cali brought back so many unwanted memories. The last time I saw him, he was rolling me out of his car in front of the hospital after he shot me. I looked over at him and saw his eyebrows started to crease as he exhaled loudly.

"Aight, I'm on my way there now," he said hanging up the phone, now visibly upset.

"Everything ok?" I asked.

"Yea, I just have to make a stop somewhere. If you don't mind, it's kind of an emergency." A little nervous that this may have something to do with Cali, I still agreed to go along with him. I didn't have to be back at the house until one anyway, and Kianni's basketball practice didn't start until two.

"Cool, I didn't want to take you home anyway. You ain't about to take that nap without me," he said.

"That's fine, you can sleep on the couch," I said.

"Messed up," he sighed, as he pulled on to Auburn Street. I was confused as to what we were doing in this neck of the woods. I wasn't too beat to be out here. The last time I was in this area was seven years ago, when I was getting high. The motel I used to trick from wasn't too far from here either.

"You can stay in the car, I won't be too long. I'm just running in to get someone and coming right back out. This area isn't as bad as it looks," he said.

"I'm pretty familiar with the area, I'll be fine," I said, looking up at him.

"What you doing be familiar with this area?" he asked.

"You are so nosey. Just go in and do what you need to do. I'll be here when you get back," I said, pushing him out the car door.

When he got out the car, I started thinking about how much my life had changed. I went from being in love with a baller to getting addicted to heroin, to being shot, to stripping and being a mom. I'd been through hell and I'm convinced you can't get no lower than where I've been. The only way to go now is up. I pulled out my phone and sent Saniyah a text,

137

telling her I should be there in an hour. Seconds later, she sent me a text back saying her and Kianni was at her mom's house. I felt a little better after hearing that. I was a little concerned that Kianni was probably driving her crazy right now, but Shaniyah's mom loved Kianni, so he was probably with her. I put my phone away and was about to lay my head on the headrest, when I noticed John come out of, what I know for sure is a crack house, carrying a woman. He was walking towards the car with her in his arms. I jumped out and opened the door for him.

When he got to the car he gently laid her down in the back seat and shut the door. I went around and got back in the passenger seat, as he got in the driver's seat and pulled off. I sat there quietly waiting for him to say something, but he didn't.

"Are you going to take her to the hospital?" I asked him as I picked at my nails.

"Nah, I'm just going to take her back to my house," he said.

"Back? She lives with you?" I asked.

"Not really, I just let her stay there every once in the while." *Every once in a while*, I thought to myself. Now I was curious as to whom this girl was, but I wasn't going to ask.

"Oh, ok. You can drop me off at my car," I said to him.

"You done hanging with me for the day?" he asked.

"You have things to handle," I said, pointing in the back seat. I continued to nervously pick at my nails and I could feel him staring at me.

"You right," he said, looking in the rearview mirror. Five minutes later, we were pulling into Velour's parking lot. He parked next to my car and turned the car off.

"Will I see you at practice today, Kandice?" he asked.

"Maybe, depends on how much sleep I can get in before practice," I said.

"Good. I had fun with you, Kandice. Have a good nap."

"Thanks, enjoy the rest your day," I responded, reaching over and kissing him on the lips. I tried to move back to my seat, but he held on to my face and stuck his tongue inside my mouth, and tongue kissed me for what felt like forever.

"Oh here," he said, reaching in his pocket and taking out a stack of money. He handed me a hundred-dollar bill.

"What's this for?"

"For baby girl. I told her I would pay her. Tell her we might need her services again real soon. Like tomorrow night."

"Oh really?"

"Yes, really. I ain't done with you yet, Ms. Kandice," he said. I smiled and shook my head.

"Bye," I said, getting out the car and shutting the door. I looked in the back seat and the girl eyes were open, but she shut them back quickly. She must've thought I ain't see that shit. I drove straight to Saniyah's house to pick up my baby boy.

When I got to Saniyah's house, I knocked on the door and I walked straight in like I always did. Her mom and I had gotten pretty cool since Saniyah been watching Kianni.

"Where my baby boy at?" I asked as I walked into the house. I could hear his feet on the hardwood floors as he came running down the hall towards me. When I rounded the corner, I scooped him up and started planting kisses all over his face.

"Mommy missed you, lil' man," I said, as I hugged him tight and swung him from side to side.

"Mommy, put me down," he laughed.

"But I missed you," I whined.

"I missed you too, Mommy. Now can you put me down."

"Fine," I said, putting him back down. He picked up the basketball and started bouncing it.

"Kianni, what I tell you about that ball?" Stephany yelled from the other room.

"Ooh, you in trouble," I said, walking into the other room.

"Hey, boo," I greeted, walking into the living room, giving Stephany a hug.

"Where's my girl?" I asked her.

"She's back there. Saniyah," she called as I sit down on the couch, cuddling with a pillow. I shut my eyes for a minute.

"Hey, Ms. Kandice," she said, coming into the living room.

"Hey, babes. Huh, this from your new friend," I said, handing her the money.

"Balling," she said, taking the money from me.

"So how was your date?"

"It was great. He was great. He wants to take me out again tomorrow night. Will you be able to watch Kianni?"

"Who's asking? You or him?" she inquired.

"He is."

"Well, then tell him I'm charging him by the hour. I'll draw him a bill up by the time he returns you home," she said, turned around and headed back to her room. I couldn't help but laugh. Like I said, Saniyah was about her money.

"So who is this man?" Stephany asked as I cuddled back up with the pillow.

"Kianni's basketball coach, John"

"Where did he take you?

"All the way to AC, girl."

"Nice... did you give him some?"

"What? You so nosey. What in your right mind would make you think I would give him some?"

"I'm just asking. Well did you?"

"None of your business, nosey," I said, closing my eyes and

smiling, thinking about my wonderful morning.

"Something done happened that got you over there smiling like that. It's cool you want to hold back the tea. I got you." That was the last thing I heard before I was being awakened by Kianni shaking me.

"Mommy, it's time for practice," Kianni said.

"Oh shit!" I jumped up and looked at the clock. It was two o'clock.

"I can drop him off, but I can't stay," Stephany said.

"Oh please, I just need to run home and take a shower. It'll only take me like 20 minutes. Just let his coaches know I'll be there." I said.

"No problem. Come Ki, let's get up out of here," she said, grabbing her keys and her purse. I started putting my shoes on and ran out the door, jumped in my car and drove home.

Chapter 14

Pepper

"Bitch, you lying," I said, responding to Keisha's story about her stepping to Kandi.

"If I'm lying then I'm motherfucking flying. I was about to beat that bitch's ass up in that dressing room, trying to act like she cared and shit. If it wasn't for Big Mike's ass, I would've stomped that bitch out so bad I would have had her stuck to the bottom of my shoe like a piece of discarded gum."

"Yea right, Kandi would have killed ya punk ass. We all know you ain't shit without me being there.

"What was yo' ass doing out in VA anyway?"

"I went out there with my boo," I said.

"Who's your boo, bitch? You know the rules. Ya ass don't go home or no damn road trips with no damn nigga without you sending me his name, number, address, birthday, social security number, license plate number, his momma and daddy info, I want everything," she said, running off her nigga checklist.

"Tech. You know the nigga that's at the club almost every weekend, throwing big bucks."

"Oh yea, that nigga is fine. He got a brother or father? Shit, I'll even take a sister if he has one."

"Hell yea, girl, he got a sexy ass brother, John. I can probably get you the hook up," I said.

"Oh hell yea. Make that happen."

"Who you on the phone with?" Tech came in the room asking. He flopped down on the bed and snatched the phone out my hand.

"Who this?" he asked.

"Who the hell is this?" Keisha responded.

"Give me my damn phone. It's my girl, Keisha," I said, snatching my phone back.

"She wanna know what's good with ya brother," I said, trying to hook her up.

"What you mean, what's good with my brother?"

"Is he single?"

"Yea, why you asking?" his slow ass asked.

"Keisha trying to get at him."

"He don't want her. I can tell by her voice she ain't his type."

"What you mean you can tell by my voice?" Keisha asked from the other end of the phone.

"I can tell yo' ass is ratchet and ghetto, and he ain't about that shit. He like them uppity hoes. The dignified ones, but I ain't gonna stop you. Next time you see him, holla at him; you never know, he might just give you a chance."

"Alright, I will. P, I'll call you tomorrow. I'll leave you two alone," she said, hanging up the phone.

"Hey, baby." I put my phone down on the dresser.

"How you feeling?" he asked.

"I have a little pain, but it's nothing that good ole perc can't handle. What you about to do?" I asked him.

"I have to practice in a bit. I coach a few little shorties from the block."

"Which sport do you coach?"

"I coach basketball, hun. Well, I'm the assistant coach, my brother is the head coach. This is his team," he said.

"That's nice of you guys helping out the community. I wish there were some kind of big brother, big sister programs around when I was younger. Maybe I wouldn't be in the predicament I'm in now."

"What predicament is that?"

"Shaking my ass for money," I said.

"Oh yeah?" he asked.

"Yes, Coach Tech. I wish there were coaches like you when I was younger. I have a little friend that needs some coaching right now," I said, as I crawl over to the side of the bed where he was lying. I pushed him with my good arm so that he was now laying on his back. I climbed on top of him, then reached down and placed a kiss on his lips.

"I have something for you," he said, digging inside the pockets of his shorts and he pulled out a red box and handed it to me.

"What's this for?" I asked.

"This is for helping my brother out. If you weren't there, who knows what would have happened. I owe you and so does he, so this is part of me showing my appreciation," he said.

I opened up the box and there were some beautiful diamond studs inside.

"These are beautiful baby, thank you," I said, reaching down and kissing him on the lips again, this time sticking my hand down his shorts and grabbing his dick.

"Are you trying to start something?" he asked.

"Yep, I sure I am," I said.

"Ok, but let's make this quick. Can't leave the kiddies waiting while Coach Tech get his freak on," he said, as he rolled on top of me and effortlessly slid my shorts off.

Johnathan

"Ok, who's up for a 5-on-5 game?" I asked my players. I haven't slept in 24 hours, but I still managed to make it here for practice. Part of my reason for coming was hopes of seeing Kandi's face again. Tech and I split the boys up into two teams. I was a little upset to see Kianni there and not Kandi. She was tired so I assumed she was napping.

"Alright boys, let's get it started," I said, blowing the whistle as they started the game. I sat down on the bench and watched the games. These boys were really getting it in, going shot for shot with one another. I felt like a proud coach because at the end of the day, no matter who won, both teams were my boys and I coached them. I looked up and around the gym, and in walked probably the most beautiful woman alive. I guess she decided to come after all. Walking by, she had every nigga in the gym breaking their necks to watch her. The jeans she had on was fitting her so tight it was like a second layer of skin. Her thick thighs, hips and ass were the perfect ratio from each other. She had on one of those white half shirts that showed her toned belly and perfect C cups. I never noticed the tattoo she had going down the spine of her back. I guess she had it covered up when she danced. Her curly hair was pulled back in a ponytail, and on her face was nothing but lip gloss. She was an effortless beauty. She sat down in the bleachers and started watching the game. She made eye contact with me and I gave her a head nod and she waved at me. I smiled and went back to watching the game. The shit started getting good; it felt like it was a real game. You had parents yelling and 'ooos' and 'ahhhhs'. You would have thought it was a NBA game going on instead of a bunch of 5, 6, 7 and 8-year-olds.

"That's right, baby," Kandice yelled as Kianni went up for the layup. She was now out of her seat, and running up and down the court, following the game. It was getting hella intense in here. At the end of game, the team Kianni was on lost. The other kids on his team were nice, but at the end of the day, it seemed like Kianni was carrying the team on his own.

"Good practice, clap it up," I said as they all huddled in a circle.

"Hands in everyone," I said as they all put in their hands. Tech started counting off.

"One, two, three, All Stars," we all said as they all started to scatter to their parents. I went and collected all the equipment. When I was done, I looked in the bleachers and my blood started to boil at the sight of Cali in Kandice's face.

Kandi

The sight of Cali made me throw up in my mouth twice, and swallow it both times. Why was I looking at this man right now? He ruined my life and I prayed to God that I would never see him again. I tried walking around him, but he grabbed me by my arm.

"Where you going, Kandi, baby?" he asked me.

"As far away from you as I can get," I said, snatching my arm away from him.

"You looking good, Kandi. You look like the little girl I picked up nine years ago. I miss you Kandi, you don't miss me?" he asked as John and Kianni came over.

"Fuck you doing here, nigga? You must wanna die today, motherfucker," John said, getting up in Cali's face. I was a little confused as to what was really going on right now.

"Mommy, you ready to go?" Kianni asked, grabbing on to my hand.

"Yes, baby, let's get out of here."

"Mommy? This yo' kid, Kandi?"

"Her name is Kandice not Kandi," Kianni said, defending his mommy.

"Wow, Kandi, I mean Kandice. Hey little man, you know me and your momma were friends, way back in the day. How old are you exactly?" Cali asked.

"Don't you even try it," I said, pulling Kianni behind me. I already knew what he was trying to get at. He was trying to insinuate that Kianni may have been his kid, but that wasn't even close to being accurate.

"I'm just making sure," he said about to put his hand on Kianni's head, but I reached and tried to smack it away. However, Johnathan got to it before me and I ended up smacking his arm.

"My bad, babe," I apologized.

"Why the fuck you in my gym, nigga? Ya pussy ass set us up and almost had me and my brother killed and got his shawty shot. Nigga, I promise you if we weren't in this gym with all these kids I would blow ya shit off," John said, placing two of his fingers to the top of Cali's head. Two of the men that came in with Cali started walking up the bleachers. Cali held up his hand and they stopped.

"You officially used up all of your disrespect passes. I think it's about time you start respecting your elders, little boy. Now I get your upset, but that wasn't supposed to go down like that. It was supposed to be a drop off and that's it. That nigga wasn't supposed to check the product."

"Wait, I'm not sure what's going on here, but Kianni are I leaving. John, call me later," I said, touching his arm.

"Oh, ok, I see what's going on here. I know your secrets, Kandi. I'll see you around, you'll be mine again," he said, as I walked out the door of the gym. I knew John was going to have a few questions for me next time we spoke.

Johnathan

"Wait, did he just say Kandi as in Kandi from the club? Oh shit. Kandice is Kandi? No wonder why she looked so familiar," Tech said.

"Not now, nigga," I said to him.

"This little arrangement we got is done. Find someone else to run ya shit, now get the fuck out my gym before I kill you and your fucking apes over there," I said, getting in Cali's face. I had a lot animosity, hate, and anger built up against this man. From my suspicions of him killing Previous, to him

153

setting us up, to the interaction he just had with Kandi. I really wanted to know what that was about, but I wasn't going to overstep my boundaries by questioning Kandice's past.

"Little nigga, get the fuck out my face," Cali said, pushing me. I stumbled because I was standing on the bleachers. The next thing I heard was guns being cocked. I looked up and Tech had the burner to the middle of Cali's forehead and Cali's men had their guns pointed at Tech.

"Come on, bro. It's all good. Here ain't the place for this," I said, pulling Tech back, looking around the gym.

"I hope you punk niggas ain't expecting a payment. That shit is a done deal," Cali said.

"It's all good. We took our payment back in Virginia and bodied a nigga or two. Guess who they gon' come looking for? You. Guess what we did with ya product? Tossed that shit in the Passaic River," I said with a smile. The smug look on his face started to fade and you could tell he was bothered.

"You motherfuckers will pay for this shit, I promise you. Watch ya back," he said as he walked down the bleachers and his two goons followed him.

"I wanna kill that nigga so bad I can taste it," Tech said.

"We will, bro. But we need to plan better and catch that nigga while he's slipping. Let's get out of here," I said, as we left out and locked up the gym. I got in the car and made my way home. I was tired as a bitch.

Chapter 15

Two Days Later

Johnathan

I pulled up to Kandice's apartment and texted her to let her know I was downstairs. I laid my head back in the seat as I rapped the lyrics to Jay's verse on "I Got the Keys" by DJ Khaled.

Niggas always asking me the key
'Til you own your own you can't be free
'Til you're on your own you can't be me
How we still slaves in 2016?
Key to life, keep a bag comin'
Every night another bag comin'
I ain't been asleep since '96
I ain't seen the back of my eyelids
I been speeding' through life with no safety belt
One on one with the corner, with no safety help.

Saniyah came out the building and ran up to the car.

"Hey, John," she said, leaning in the window.

"Hey, baby girl. How doing today?"

"I'm doing pretty good, just hungry," she said. I laughed and reached in the back of the car.

"Here you go, little lady." I handed her the bag of food I had picked up for them.

"Now this is what I'm talking about. Hot Grill on deck. Ms. Kandice told you I wanted Hot Grill, didn't she?"

"Yea, she did. And this is for you too," I said handing her a 100-dollar bill.

"This is too much. I only charge Ms. Kandice fifty a night."

"Yea, I know, but she also told me you saving up for a car, so this will help you out a little," I said.

"Thanks, John. You seem like a really nice guy. Ms. Kandice is really lucky to find someone like you, and you, her. She's a really beautiful person inside and out, don't hurt her, ok Coach John?" Saniyah said.

"I promise she's in good hands. Here, take these upstairs for her," I said, handing her a dozen of roses.

"And here these are for you," I said, reaching in the back again, handing her a bouquet of assorted wildflowers I picked up from Shop Rite earlier when I went to visit my mom's grave.

"These are for me," she said, blushing like the school girl she was.

"Yup. Now go tell Ms. Kandice to hurry before I come up there and get her."

"Ok. Wait until you see her, she's looks really nice. I helped her pick out her outfit. Thanks for the flowers," she said as she ran back into the building. I sat my chair back little, pulled out my phone, and started looking through my calendar. I had two trips scheduled, one for Washington and another to Maryland. That's when I realized that I had to go fuel the buses up before my drivers come in tomorrow. The other day in AC, I had made sure to store Kandice's birthday in here too. I wanted to do something nice for her. I wanted it to be a surprise, so I had to somehow get in touch with Saniyah without Kandice knowing.

I sat in the car for five more minutes before Kandice appeared in the lobby of her building. I could see her through the glass doors and Saniyah was right. She looked good as fuck. I didn't even realize my mouth was open until I felt drool roll from my mouth and down my chin. I wiped at it as I continued to watch her strut out the door. She had on a navy blue dress that had a flower pattern that stopped mid-thigh. It wasn't too tight but fitted enough that it showed off her figure. When she turned around to shut the door, the back of the dress was dipped low just above her ass, which showed off her toned back and that sexy ass tattoo that ran down her spine. She had on pink open toe shoes with white nail polish. It was something about a white toenail that made my dick jump at the sight of it. Her hair was wild and curly as if she had taken braids out and left it like that. I got out the car and met her halfway.

"Hey, beautiful," I said, walking up to her.

"Hey, handsome," she responded with a kiss on the cheek.

"You look gorgeous, had a nigga slobbing in the car and everything.

"Well, thank you. I had to match ya fly, boo," she said as we walked to the car. I couldn't help but watch her ass as I walked behind her. All I could think about was pleasuring her all night, but that wasn't going to happen tonight. I really was feeling Kandice. I didn't want her to think it was only about sex. I opened the car door and let her get inside.

"I think you about to be someone's Man Crush Monday," she said.

"What you talking about?" I asked her.

"I'm talking about Saniyah. You got her upstairs all cheesy from the flowers you gave her."

"Oh," I said, laughing.

"So where are we going?" she asked as I got in the car.

"Jersey City, baby girl," I responded. "The Vu."

"I have no idea where that is, but as long as they have drinks, I'm down," she said.

"Long day?"

"Job hunting has me stressed," she said.

"You know if you really want a job I can give you one."

"Where?"

"I told you I own a charter bus company, I could use someone to do booking, advertising, scheduling services for the bus. Just say the word and you have a job."

"How much you paying? Don't be trying to cheat me because we're friends."

"I wouldn't do that girl, stop playing. What's your desired salary?" I asked her.

"I don't really know. I never really had a job besides the club."

"What's your highest education level?"

"I have my high school diploma, that's it."

"I'll show you what to do and later when you get home, you come up with a salary and let me know. Don't be shy with the numbers, sweetheart."

"Ok," she smiled.

I turned up the radio as I cruised down Highway 20. I turned back to "I Got The Keys". As I was driving, from the corner of my eyes, I could see Kandice's head bobbing to the music.

"What you know about this?" I asked her.

"What? I got the keys, keys, keys," she rapped as she milly

161

rocked to the beat.

"You ratchet as hell," I said, laughing at her.

"Whatever, this my shit," she said, sitting back in her seat and enjoying the rest of the ride.

Kandi

"You want another drink, beautiful?" Johnathan asked me.

"Yes, please," I responded giggly. I was really enjoying my night. The night was perfect, the lounge was perfect, the view of the Hudson River, and the New York skyline was perfect, and best of all, my date was perfect, not to mention sexy as fuck. Those bedroom eyes had my kitty on purr. It could have also been these damn drinks too. I was too tipsy, but I felt good.

"Yea, let me get another one of those Peach Blossoms and a glass of water, please," Johnathan said to the waitress who was standing there with a notepad and pen. She was smiling a little too hard at him. Even after he ordered the drinks, home girl was still standing there staring at him.

"That'll be all," I said, interrupting her daydream. She looked at me and turned and walked away. Johnathan sat there laughing.

"What was all of that?" he asked.

"She sitting there staring at you like she was ready to sit on your face. Now what if I was your girl? I would have felt straight disrespected and I would have had to make her swallow those eyeballs whole." He started laughing again.

"You laugh all you want, don't be the cause of a bitch's death."

"You said if I was your man. Am I your man?" he asked as he played with a balled up piece of paper.

"No you're not, but so what, I'll still smack a heffa for disrespecting me whether you're my man or not."

"How can we make that possible?" he asked.

"Make what possible? A bitch getting slapped?"

"No, me being your man."

"You're on the right track," I said, blushing.

"This is good to know," he said as the waitress brought our drinks back.

"You really only got a water? You whack."

"I wanna be sober so that I can remember this night with you and how incredible you look," he said, making my panties wet. He just might get some tonight.

After I finished off my drinks, I was in the mood to dance. Johnathan said he knew a place where I could go dance. We pulled up to Bliss Lounge 20 minutes later, and we jumped out the car. When we got inside, we went straight to VIP.

"Bro, what's good?" he said, walking up to his brother, Tech.

"Shit, we just came from dinner, figured we would come check shit out."

"That's what's up. How you doing Ms. Kandice?" Tech said.

"I'm pretty good, how are you?" I responded.

"I'm pretty drunk," he said.

"Aye, let me introduce you to my boo thang, Pepper. If I'm not mistaken the two of you know each other already."

"Yea, we know each other already. Hey Pepper, how you feeling?" I asked her.

"Like I just got shot. Oh wait, I did," she said, laughing.

She was beyond intoxicated. She could barely stand up.

"Okay, what the hell was she drinking?" I asked Tech.

"Everything you see on this table," Tech said, and I shook my head. Johnathan and I sat down on the chair as we both vibed to the music. I got up to go to the bathroom which took all but five minutes. When I got back, there was some chick sitting where I was sitting and she was all up in Johnathan's face. I was definitely bothered by it, but I wasn't going to let it show. I picked up my drink and sat down in the chair across from them. When John finally realized I was sitting there, he looked up at me and smiled.

"Why you sitting over there?" he asked.

"I didn't want to be rude and ruin your conversation."

"You're worth the distraction, baby girl," he said, doing that eye squinting thing he does that makes my coochie want to detach from my body and bite him. He waved his hand for me to come over there. I walked over there and sat on his lap, not paying the other chick no mind.

"I knew yo' ass was a hoe. Walking around here like you

165

better than everybody." I turned around, recognizing the voice.

"I'm not better than everyone, but I know for sure I'm better than you, boo," I said to Keisha, Pepper's best friend.

"The only thing you may be better at is keeping ya hoeing under wraps, sweetie."

"Let me tell you something, sweetheart. You got one more time to call me a hoe and I will slap the black off yo' ass. I'm sick of yo' hating ass starting shit with me when I don't say two words to you," I said, standing up off Johnathan's lap. He stood up in front of me.

"It's all good, baby, let's go dance." He pushed me towards the dance floor.

"This the second time someone done saved you from death," I said as I walked down the steps to the dance floor with John holding me by my waist.

When we got to the dance floor, "Luv" by Tory Lanez was on. This was my shit. He still had me by my waist and it felt as if he wasn't ever letting go, so I started winding my waist against him. He kept holding my skirt down so that it wouldn't come up, but I had sprayed fabric glue on my thighs so that it wouldn't rise. He let my dress go and grabbed onto my hands, then turned me around to face him. He held me close to his body as I continued to wind and grind on him. He matched my rhythm as we both locked lips and kissed on the dance floor. I don't know how long we were kissing for, but we were distracted by someone's loud, dry ass hands clapping in our ears. We both turned our attention to that person and I wish I hadn't.

"You two looking mighty cozy," Cali said. I gave him the talk to the hands gesture and attempted to walk away, but he grabbed me by the arm.

"Get ya fucking hands off me, Cali," I said, snatching away from him.

"Bitch," he said just as a fist came across his face, which sent him stumbling into his two friends behind him. The two guys pushed Cali in back of them, and they both started jumping on Johnathan. I looked on the floor for the Corona bottle I had kicked with my foot when we first got to the dance floor. I went and picked it up and slammed it across one of the guy's head. He stumbled backwards about to fall on me, but I was able to move out the way just in time. I looked over at Johnathan and he was going blow for blow with the other guy,

167

who was twice his size. I was on my way over there to help him when someone started tugging on my hair. I started swinging on whoever it was. This person was strong as shit. I looked up and it was Cali's bitch ass. I grabbed on to his hand to prevent him from pulling anymore, because it felt like he was snatching my hair right out of my head. He continued to yank at it, so I kicked him straight in his dick and he went down to the ground, letting my hair go. I turned around looking for Johnathan, and him and Tech were over there beating the shit out of the other guy. I sat there watching the fight with the rest of the crowd, when gunshots started ringing out.

I ducked for cover as everyone started to scatter. I was getting knocked over every time I tried to get up. I somehow got lost in the crowd and was now being pushed towards the door. When I got outside, I walked over to Johnathan's car and waited there for him.

"See what the fuck you done started, bitch," Keisha said, walking past the car. Pepper was with her.

"You alright, Kandi?" Pepper asked.

"It's Kandice, and yes, I'm alright, thanks," I said.

"Bitch, ya name is Kandi, you're a stripper, and always going to be a stripper. Stop trying to act all bourgeois like ya shit don't stink when in fact ya pussy gets sweaty like the rest of us."

I was fed up with this bitch. I reached and grabbed that bitch by the lips with my left hand, and punched the bitch in the face with my right. She fell to the ground.

"Ain't nobody here to save yo' ass now, bitch," I said, as I started stomping her with my heels. She grabbed onto my foot and pulled me down to the ground with her. I climbed on top of her and started delivering blows to her face. She started pulling my hair and I became pissed. I was sick of people pulling my hair today. I grabbed the side of her head and started slamming it into the concrete.

"Kandi, stop," Pepper said trying to stop me, but she was down an arm so she couldn't really do much. I felt myself being lift up in the air, but that didn't stop me from swinging.

"Calm down, baby girl," I heard John's voice. I immediately became calm. I turned around and hugged him.

"You're ok! I was worried about you," I said to him.

"I'm good, Ma. Let's get up out of here," he said, opening

the door for me to get in. Tech and Pepper were helping ole girl off the floor. I really hated that bitch, Keisha. If I was driving, that hoe would be under my car. I rolled down the window, took the water bottle out the cup holder, and threw it at that bitch, hitting her right in that big ass mouth of hers.

"Oh shit," Johnathan said.

"Dumb hoe," I said, sitting back in the seat and putting my seat belt on.

"You mad crazy, baby girl," he said while laughing at me.

"Shit ain't funny," I said, turning towards him. That's when I noticed the cut above his eye.

"Oh my God, are you ok?"

"Yea, I'm good. This ain't shit, man."

"Go to my house, I have a first aid kit in my car."

"I have one at my house, it's closer than your place," he said.

"Ok," I agreed.

We got to his house in no more than five minutes. It really was close as hell to the club. We pulled up into the driveway and the sight of his house blew me away.

"What the hell is a 25-year-old doing with a house this big?" I asked him, sitting up in my seat to take in the rest of the house. He laughed at me.

"I told you, baby girl, age ain't nothing but a number. I have goals that I started chasing at a young age. I meant that shit when I told you, I wasn't nothing like them other young ass niggas running the streets. I'm focused on my future. Shit, more like obsessed with it."

"I see," I responded.

"Come on, get out. Let's go clean that hand up," he said, nodding towards my hand. I looked down at my hands. I never even realized that I had a cut on one of them. More like a scrape. Probably scraped it across the ground when I was fighting Keisha's black ass.

We got out the car, walked up to the house, and he unlocked the door and allowed me to walk in first. As soon as I walked in, I smelled something, something way too familiar.

"What's that smell?" I asked.

"What smell?" he asked, sniffing the air.

"There's a smell in here, Johnathan. Someone else lives here with you?" I asked walking further into the house.

"Not permanently, just temporarily."

"Is it that girl you picked up the other day?"

"Yea, she here, but there's nothing going on between us," he said.

"Oh, ok," I said.

"Ok, what?"

"I know what the smell is now."

"Oook, you care to share?" he asked. I looked over at him.

"Venom," I said. He looked at me, probably curious as to how I knew that.

"Hold the hell up, I know damn well she ain't..." he said, jogging up the stairs. I followed right behind him; I wanted to see more of the house. When we got up to the second level of the house, he walked down the hall fast. He walked down to the last bedroom at the end of the hall and pushed the door open and went in. I stood outside the door for a minute as he searched the room. He opened the bathroom and went in. I heard smacking sounds and then the shower came on. I walked in and surveyed the scene before me. There was a slight moment where I froze as memories of me getting stupid high and passing out anywhere and tricking, stealing, and getting shot, started flooding my mind.

"That's not going to work, Johnathan."

"What?" he said from the shower as he stood in there with the girl getting his clothes wet as he held her under the water. She had to be someone he cared about. I could tell just by the way he stroked her hair.

"You know what, I'm going to go," I said, turning to leave.

"No you not. Come hand me that towel right there," he said, pointing at the towel rack on the wall. I did as he asked and just stood there. I reached over and cut the water off.

"Why you cut the water off?"

"Because, that's not going to work. You just have to let her sleep it off, John," I said, reaching over and checking her pulse.

"How do you know?" he asked.

"I just do." I ran over and got more towels and helped dry her off. He carried her out the tub and into the bedroom where I had towels laid out on the bed so that it wouldn't get wet when he laid her down.

"Does she have clothes here?" I asked him.

"Yes, she does," he said, running out the room. I walked over to her and lifted the sleeves of her shirt up and I felt like crying. I pulled them both back down as I heard Johnathan coming back down the hallway.

"Here you go," he said, sitting them on the bed.

"I have a question?"

"Ok," he said.

"Who is she to you?" I asked him. I needed to know before I started undressing her.

"She's my ex-fiancée."

"I don't know if you want to be in here when I start undressing her. It's not a pretty sight under these clothes."

"I'm good, don't worry about me," he said. I wasn't going to keep fighting him. I warned him. I turned back around to her and started to remove her clothes. The sight of the open needle marks that covered her arms and legs sent a lonely tear down my cheek, at the same time it turned my stomach. The injection ulcers were the sizes of dimes and they were going down both arms and legs. All I could think about was that this could have been me. From the sight of her body, she had to shoot up every hour of the day for some years now. There was no visible or available vein for her to use. How the hell was she getting high? I started removing her underwear and she had ulcers in her pubic area as well. She needed to get treated ASAP or she might die of some kind of infection. I felt Johnathan come up behind me and look over my shoulder.

"Oh hell fuckin no," he said as he walked out the room, slamming the door behind him. I warned him. This may have just scarred him for life. I finished removing her clothes and started redressing her. I placed the shirt over her head. I looked up at her and her eyes were all of a sudden opened and that shit scared the hell out of me. She was looking at me. Probably trying to wonder who I am.

"Hey, I'm Kandice, a friend of Johnathan's." She continued to look at me not blinking once. Then she rolled her eyes and turned over in the bed.

"Excuse the fuck out of me," I said low, as I collected the wet clothes and walked out the room, shutting the door.

Johnathan

I was sitting on the couch downstairs when Kandice came walking down the stairs.

"I know there's a laundry room somewhere in the big ass house," she said. I pointed to the door that led to the basement where the laundry was. I sat there thinking about what I had just seen. I wish I had just walked out when Kandice told me to. Reality had really just set in that my Kori was really an addict. I don't think there was any coming back for her. Maybe I did need to take her ass back to rehab and just be done with her once and for all. I mean she done got me for a good 30 grand with all the shit she done stole and pawned. That includes the 20-thousand-dollar engagement ring I got for her.

Kandice came walking back into the room. I tapped the couch for her to come sit down next me. I placed my arm around her and pulled her closer, and we just sat there silently for a bit.

"How you feeling?" she asked me.

"Disgusted," I answered honestly.

"You should probably take her to a hospital or something. The open lesions are going to start getting really infected."

"Fuck that shit. I should throw her ass out on her ass. I can't believe she allowed herself to get that bad. I tried helping her so many times and seeing that, I realized it's really a waste of my time," I said, meaning every word. Kandice sat there quietly as she listened to my rant. I know it was a little too early to be showing her my temper. The room got quiet again. I sat there thinking if it was the right time to start digging at her. I had a lot of questions for her. Shit, I might as well go on and ask her now.

"Can I ask you questions?" I asked her. I felt her body start to tense up.

"Sure," she said and you could hear the nervousness in her voice.

"Ok, sit up," I said, turning towards her. I looked her in her face and for some reason, she couldn't look me back in my face. I had never seen a vulnerable side of Kandice. Even the night at the club when that nigga, June, attacked her, she was crying but it was anger, not a scared cry.

"You were able to identify Venom usage just through the smell and I honestly didn't smell anything. How is that? And how is it that you were so calm when you saw those marks on her body, and you knew that the water wasn't going to work and when I asked how did you know, you said you just do? How do you know, Kandice? Did you go through this with a relative or something?" She looked up at me and then looked away.

"I used to be her. Although not as bad, but I, too, was hooked on to Venom seven years ago. I was a heroin addict," she said as tears fell from her eyes.

"Two years before I had Kianni, I was involved with this guy who was a heavy drug dealer and he introduced me to it. He used to pump me up with the stuff all the time, to a point where I started pumping myself up. I was young and naive and thought this guy was the love of my life, and he turned out to be nothing but a piece of shit. One day, he came home with a new woman, someone younger than me. Someone who he could turn out. He replaced me and put me out on my ass, literally. He threw me out that door naked, scrapped my ass all up. When I was with this guy, I had all the Venom I could ever want. Without this guy, I did what I had to, to get high. I started tricking for money to buy drugs, but that stopped when I was attacked by one of the johns. I tried robbing people, but that didn't go too well. You see this," she said turning around and point to a scar on her back.

"I was shot when I broke into the guy's house I was messing with, and tried to rob him. He shot me in the back and then rolled me out of his car in front of the hospital. I thought I was going to die. I thought my life was over, but for some odd reason, the man above saved me. After I got out the hospital, I checked myself into rehab where I got clean and felt like I was ready to reenter the world. I got a job working at Velour and that's where I have been for the last five years until I got fired."

"Wow... It's so hard to believe that you been through all that, Ma. I'm sorry but I'm happy you got through it. Your strength is incredible. I applaud you," I said, lifting up her chin so that she could look me in my eyes. I wanted her to know that she had nothing to be ashamed of.

"So how do you know, Cali?" I asked her. She let out a little laugh.

"Cali was that guy," she said, looking up at me. Now it all made sense why she hated his guts so much. Now I was really determined to murder that fucker.

"Come here, Ma," I said, pulling her over to me so she could lay on my chest. I rubbed her back as we continued to talk.

"Now you see why I hate that nigga, Cali, so much? If I got the chance I would piss on his grave," she said.

"Hearing what he did to you, I just might make that happen for you, Ma. Is he Kianni's father?"

"No, he's not," she sighed.

"The person who impregnated me without my permission hopefully bled out in his office the other day," she said.

"Wait, hold up. What you mean without your permission?"

"Meaning, back then after I got of rehab, no one wanted to hire me. I needed to survive, so I auditioned for June. When the audition was done, he took me to his office where he offered me the job only if I slept with him. I was desperate so I did it. At the start of it, I made him put a condom on but by the end, he had somehow taken it off. He wanted me to get an abortion, but didn't want to give me the money for it, so I kept him. June is married, so in order for me to keep my mouth shut and not go to child support, he paid me a little more than the other girls and gives me money every two weeks, although that is probably going to stop since I stabbed him."

"Damn girl, you can't get away from pussy ass niggas, huh?" She laughed.

"Do you consider yourself a pussy ass nigga?" she asked me.

"Do you think I'm a pussy nigga?"

"No, I think you're pretty badass. Especially the way you beat that dude up in the club."

"No, you busting homeboy in the head with a bottle was badass."

"Well, you know I'm a bad bitch."

"You most certainly are, baby girl," I said, smacking her ass.

"Boy, you better stop before you start something you can't finish," she said talking shit.

"Yea, aight. I'll have ya ass tapping out, playing with me."

"Whatever, little boy," she said, standing up. I grabbed her by her arm, pulling her back on the couch. I got between her legs and started kissing her on the lips. I slid my hands up her thighs and under her dress, gripping on to her ass as I kissed her deeply, and she returned the same passion. I sat up on my knees and lifted both of her legs. I slid her panties off her ass and up her legs, taking them off. I kissed down her calves and her thighs and kissed both ass cheeks. I spread her legs and was now looking down at her clean shaven strawberry Starburst. I couldn't wait to dive in and that's what I did. Just like last time, that shit tasted so amazing, I almost wanted to start chewing and swallowing her shit. Her moans alone made me start slurping at her gushy pussy.

"Oh my God, you taste so good," I said.

"I know. Can I taste you now?" she asked, looking down at me.

"You can do whatever you want, baby girl," I said as I hesitantly came up from my Starburst. She pushed me on my back and laid between my legs and kissed me.

"Mmm, I do taste good," she said, referring to her juices that I still had around my mouth. She started fumbling with my belt until it opened up. She unbuttoned my pants and reached in and pulled little mister out, and put him in her mouth. Now, I was a confident nigga when it came to my size, but the way she was deep throating my shit had me a little self-conscious. It was like she was swallowing me whole and spitting me back out. The shit felt good as hell, though. Maybe the best head I've ever gotten in my life. I let a moan escape my mouth and I knew I had to stop her right there. She wasn't about to bitch me in my own house. I pulled her up so that she was straddling me. I pulled her dress over her head and I just sat there admiring her amazing body.

"You're so beautiful," I said to her and she smiled.

"Thank you. Do you have a condom?" she asked me. I reached in my pocket and pulled a gold wrapper out. She snatched it out my hands and immediately ripped it open. I pulled my shirt off as she climbed off me and helped me pull my pants off. When I was completely naked in nothing but my socks, she squatted down and took me into her mouth again causing me to get even harder than I already was. She stood back up and hovered over me. She placed the condom on and started to slowly lower herself down on me. I grabbed on to her waist and helped her out a little bit. I slowly entered her, and her shit was tight as hell. I don't know if it was pleasure or pain written on her face. Her kitty wrapped around me so tight I felt like I could die in the pussy. Once she was on me completely, she started moving herself up and down at a slow pace so that she could get use to my size. It had to be a while since the last time she had been penetrated. She started to become really wet which helped her move up and down on my dick. I haven't felt pussy this tight since I was in high school where I took a lot of girls' virginity. I busted quick, but I was still rock hard and ready to really get it on. I laid her on her back and started dicking her down, as I hovered over her beautiful body. I reached down and kissed her, moving from her lips to her neck, then taking a titty in my mouth. She must've liked having her titties sucked, because her pussy started to become real wet.

"Damn girl, get yo' ass over here before you stain my couch," I said, lifting her up and laying her naked body on the carpet where I continued to fuck the shit out her for the next 10 minutes. She pushed at my chest and rolled over on all fours, and shoved my dick back inside her.

"Oh shit, Kandice," I moaned as I felt myself about to nut. She was throwing her ass back so hard I had to use her waist as handle bars.

"Fuck," I yelled out as I grabbed on to her shoulders and started beating her shit up with everything I had left in me, before I busted a nut so hard. I felt like this woman just took ownership of my soul. We both laid out on the floor, trying to catch our breaths.

Kandi

I laid on the floor, ass naked and breathless. It's been a long time since I had some good sex. Even then wasn't as good as this. I was ready for some more, but I kept getting this eerie feeling of being watched. Every now and then I would look towards the stairs, but no one was there. It was only us and the ex in the house, but the ex was upstairs still knocked out. I would have heard her come down those stairs. I had my eyes on the stairs the whole time.

"Can we go to your room?" I asked.

"Sure, come on," he said, lifting me up off the floor and carrying me up the stairs. When we got to the room, he laid me on this bed as he laid between my legs.

"You didn't get the feeling that someone was watching us?" I asked him. He shrugged his shoulders.

"It probably was her," he said nonchalantly.

"Her, who? I was watching the stairs, it couldn't have been her," I said, and he laughed. I didn't see what was so funny.

"There are other ways to come down the stairs, baby girl. The room she's in has a balcony with stairs that leads to the back door of the kitchen. She could have come down and watched the show."

"Wait, what? Why are you so calm about that?" I asked him.

"I don't know. If she was watching, that shit is funny as hell. I really hope she enjoyed the show because I most definitely did," he said, as I felt him attempting to enter me again. I opened up my legs a little wider and let him enter me. He slowly pressed inside of me as he moaned in my ear which drove me wild. I rolled over on top of him and started riding him until we both were exhausted and fell asleep.

Kori

Who the fuck was this bitch and where hell did she come from? I stood in the dark kitchen watching as she fucked my ex fiancé's brains out. I wasn't feeling this shit at all. If I couldn't have Johnathan back, then nobody was about to have him. Not even her. I appreciated her for taking care of me, but it was time for her to go. I turned around and walked back out the kitchen and upstairs to my room. When I got in my room, I went around to the bed and pulled out the box that had my stash inside. I took it to the bathroom, shut the door, and sat down on the toilet. I took out the needle and the rock and so badly wanted to light the shit up, but seeing my ex getting fucked made me want him back even more than this drug. I knew he would never take me back if I was still using. I stood up and opened the toilet and stood there for a minute, before I emptied the drugs I had in there and flushed the toilet. If I wanted Johnathan back, I was going to get clean and quick. I could tell just by the way he looked at her that he was indeed feeling her, but I knew he still loved me. For years he has come to my rescue and not once given up on me. That's love.

The next morning, I woke up and went downstairs and made breakfast. Just as I was finishing, I could hear footsteps coming down the stairs. When they rounded the corner, they both stopped in their tracks surprised at the sight before them. They weren't expecting me to be standing here, let alone having cooked them breakfast.

"Good morning," I said to the both of them.

"Good morning, how are you feeling?" she spoke.

"Like I need a hit, but I'm practicing self-control. I think it's about time to get myself some help. I cooked this as a token of my appreciation for your help." Johnathan just stood there looking at me. I know he had nothing to say to me. He probably was pissed and I don't blame him. He's tried so many times to help me and all I did was steal from him.

"Well, I'm gonna go and leave you two. I promise I didn't poison it. Enjoy," I said as I walked past them and was heading upstairs.

"Hey, you're not going to eat?" Johnathan finally spoke.

"I don't have much of an appetite... side effect of the drugs. I'm going to go clean myself up and go meet the lady down at Straight and Narrow. See what kind of help they can offer me," I said.

"You should also try Eva's Village. They have a great program that can probably help you out. I actually know someone down there. I can give you the information," the Kandice girl said. I really didn't like this girl, but I was going to front and continue to smile in her face like I did.

"Ok, that'll be great," I said, turning to walk up the stairs, rolling my eyes at the same time.

Chapter 16

Kandice

"Happy birthday to you, happy birthday to you..." I was awakened by the sound of people singing. I jumped up out of bed and there stood Kianni holding a small cake, and Saniyah and Johnathan standing around him. I hated surprises, but this was one was different so I was enjoying every moment of it. I couldn't stop the tears from streaming down my face. I haven't had a birthday since I was twelve when my parents threw me a surprise birthday party.

"Awww, thank you guys," I said, making a wish and then blowing out the candles.

"What did you wish for, Mommy?" Kianni asked.

"I wished for a few things. I wished that you guys win the championship game and I wished that Saniyah is able to get her car, and I wished for a million, billion, trillion dollars," I said, tickling Kianni.

"What are you doing here, Mister?" I asked Johnathan.

"My home girl came over and let me in to bring you your cake and some birthday gifts," he said.

"Oh yay, I like birthday gifts."

"Me first, mommy," Kianni said, running out the room, and came back in with flowers and a bag. He handed it to me and I opened the bag. Inside was a pair of slippers, a bottle of baby lotion, and a bag of Kotex maxi pads. I picked them up and looked at him.

"You need them, right, Mommy?"

"Yes, but not right now. Thank you, baby," I said, laughing and kissing him on the forehead.

"Told you," he said, turning towards Saniyah and sticking his tongue out.

"He wanted to use his piggy bank money and get you something, so I took him to the dollar store and he would not leave without those Kotex. He kept saying you needed them." I laughed because I could see Kianni catching a fit in the store now.

"This is from me," Saniyah said, taking a Bath and Body Works bag from behind her back. I opened it, and it was a big candle with the matching scent plug-in air freshener.

"I know how you love your candles and smell goods."

"You know me too well. Thank you," I said, reaching up and giving her a hug.

"Next, where my gift?" I said to Johnathan as I held out my hand and he smacked it.

"Girl, I ain't get you nothing," he said.

"Lies, what's behind your back?"

"My hands."

"And what's in your hands?"

"Nothing," he said. I jumped off the bed and tried to see what was behind his back, but he kept turning. I gave up and sat back on the bed.

"Whatever. I don't want ya stinking gift anyway," I said, sitting back on the bed with my arms folded.

"Here, you big baby," he said, holding out a big square box.

"Nope, I don't want it."

"Shoot, I'll take it," Saniyah said, reaching for the box, but I grabbed it first.

"Get out of here, little girl," I said to her as I started

opening the box. When I did, I was completely speechless.

"Wooww," Saniyah said, looking down at the beautiful diamond choker.

"I'm so wearing that to my prom next year," Saniyah said.

"This is beautiful, Johnathan," I finally said. I can't even imagine how expensive this could've been. I stood up from the bed and walked over to him, and kissed him on the lips as he wrapped his arms around my waist.

"Ahh sukky sukky now," Saniyah said.

"I also have this for you," he said, handing me an envelope. I opened it and it was a card. I opened the card and some papers fell out. I paid no attention to the paper as I read the car. He had Kianni and Saniyah sign it as well. From the corner of my eyes, I could see Saniyah fidgeting. After reading the card, I looked down at what fell out and bent down and picked them up. It was four tickets to Miami. Now I understood the fidget.

"You're taking us to Miami?" I asked him.

"Yup, just for a few days. We have a championship trophy

to bring home, right Kianni?"

"Yup," he answered.

"I don't know what you're excited about, you need to ask your mom first," I said to Saniyah.

"I already did, yesterday," she said.

"You kept this from me? Ooh, the deceit. I thought we were here," I said, waving my two fingers back and forth between the two of us.

"We are here, but he told me to keep it a secret or he was going to give my ticket to the bum in front of the building."

"You didn't?" I said to him.

"I sure did."

"When do we leave?" I asked, placing my arms around his neck and kissing his lips.

"In a few, so maybe you should start packing."

"I have to pack Kianni's clothes too," I said.

"Already done," Saniyah replied.

"See, that's why he pays you the big bucks."

"You didn't have to do this for me," I said, kissing him again as we stood there hugging.

"Come on, Kianni. Let's go watch so TV until it's time to go," Saniyah said, as they walked out of the room, shutting the door.

"I wanted to do this for you," he said, as his hands started going up under my shirt. He started caressing my booty.

"You trying to start something, Coach John?"

"Maybe."

"We gotta catch that plane, sir."

"I know, but this won't take long," he said, lifting me up by my thighs and wrapping my legs around his waist. He pulled down his basketball shorts just enough to release his penis and then he moved my boy shorts over to the side. I moaned out loud as he entered my tightness.

"Shhhh," he said putting his finger over my mouth, trying to quiet me down. That was going to be hard because the feel of him inside of me was overwhelming. He continued to push inside of me as my kitty became wetter with every thrust.

195

"You feel so good, Kandice. I wish I could be in you every day," he said.

"We can probably arrange that," I said as I matched his thrusts. I rolled over on top of him and started riding him. I moaned again, as he grabbed onto my waist and started moving me back and forth.

"I'm about to cum, baby," I whispered.

"Do you, Ma," he said. Those were all the words I needed and I released. He rolled me back over and started pounding inside of me. He reached under me, wrapping his arms around my waist, as he slammed himself inside of me.

"I'm about to cum," he whispered.

"Do you," I repeated what he had to me two minutes ago. He turned his face into my neck as he moaned.

"Oh shit," he groaned as he bit down on my neck. His pace picked up and then his thrusting stopped. Everything stopped. He laid on me motionless and silently.

"Hey you, we have a plane to catch," I said.

"I need to gain my strength back. You get up and go pack," he said, moving off of me. I jumped off the bed and went into the bathroom. I sat down on the toilet to pee.

"Oh fuck," I said as I looked down at the tissue that had Johnathan's nut on it. I needed to make a stop at the pharmacy before boarding that plane. I went back into the room and started packing my clothes. I heard my cell phone ring, so I ran out of the closet and to my dresser, picking up my phone. I looked over on the bed and John was still laid out there. I laughed.

"Get yo' ass up," I said to him.

"I am, when you finish packing," he responded. I shook my head and answered my phone.

"Hello."

"Hello, baby girl," a man said from the other end of the phone.

"Who is this?"

"You don't remember your own father's voice?"

"Well, it has been a while, Dad. What you doing calling me? I thought that old bat banned you from talking to me?" I said.

"I don't care about that miserable woman. I missed my baby girl and I wanted to call you for your birthday. It's been years and I allowed your mother to dictate how to live life. She doesn't run me. I'm free to do as I feel and I wanted to hear my baby girl's voice."

"Aww, I missed you more daddy. I was always closer to you than I was to her anyway. I'm happy you called though."

"How you doing, Kandice?" my dad asked.

"I'm doing quite alright, Daddy. You know you have a grandson?" I said to my dad.

"Oh no, you're kidding me, Kandice. How come you didn't call me? I would have been there for you."

"I know you would have, but I know if I had told you and you told her, she wouldn't have allowed you to come. "

"Oh my God, Kandice, girlll. I have to meet my grandson," my dad said. I had to stop myself from laughing at my father's gay side coming out.

"Yes, you do have to meet him. He's such a wonderful kid. He plays basketball and he's really, really good, Daddy."

"We have to do lunch. How about tomorrow night?" he said.

"Umm, that won't work. A friend of mine is taking Kianni and I to Miami for a few days for my birthday. I'm not sure when we're getting back, but when we do, I'll most definitely give you a call so we can set something up."

"Ok, baby, enjoy your birthday. Turn up," he said, making me laugh.

"Ok. Bye, Daddy," I said hanging up the phone with him and went back to doing what I was doing. An hour later, we were on our way to Newark Airport.

****

Five hours later, we were inside walking into our hotel suite at the Dorchester Hotel. It was so freaking huge, way bigger than my apartment. We set the kids up in the living room area of the suite, and Johnathan and I took the bedroom. I had a feeling we were going to need a room with a door.

"So what y'all wanna do first?" Johnathan asked.

"Can we go swim with the dolphins?"

"Oh yea, that sounds like fun," I agreed. Johnathan had

199

really planned this whole thing out from activities, to him and I club hopping in VIP. Everything was beyond exciting. When it was time to go, I really didn't want to. Moving out here was definitely an option.

Chapter 17

Three weeks later

Johnathan

"Hey, Kandice, what's up?"

"Who the hell is Kandice? You're seriously mad at me right now, Johnathan? I can't believe it," she said.

"What can I do for you, Kandice?" I asked.

"You can start by not calling me Kandice. My name is baby girl to you, ok?" she said, making me crack a smile, although I really wanted to continue to be mad at her.

"I'm sorry, Johnathan. I couldn't risk getting pregnant again. I figured getting a Plan B would have been the easier way out. It was a possibility that I wouldn't have gotten pregnant anyway. Once we get a little further into our relationship, like two, maybe three years, hopefully we'll be married, and then we can try for a baby," she said. She was right though. I wasn't sure if I was ready for a baby just yet, but that should have been something her and I discussed. If I knew what I was stopping at Walgreens for when she asked, I would have kept on going straight to the airport.

"Yea, yea, yea. What's up, baby girl?"

"I'm getting a little confused over here in the office. I just need you to show me one more time and I should be good after that," she said. When we got back from Miami, I had started training her to the books and booking for me, while I handled other business. She learned fast, but every now and then, she needed me to refresh her memory. What I really think she needed was for me to dick her down some more. Every time she called talking about she forgot what to do, I would show up and we would have one big fuck-a-thon and all of a sudden she would remember.

"Did you forget or do you just need your boy to bring you this dope dick?"

"Umm, both," she said and I could hear her smiling through the phone.

"What you smiling for?"

"How you know I'm smiling?"

"Because I just have that kind of effect on women."

"You sure do. I swear ya ex tried to poison me. It was only you and I and her in the house, and all of sudden my glass of water smelled like bleach. I'm telling you, she trying to take me out," Kandice said.

"No she's not. Kori wouldn't hurt a fly. She might steal yo' shit, but she wouldn't hurt anyone."

"Yea, alright. Chicks go crazy over good dick. I'm not about to sleep on home girl. I swear she be listening to us when we're having sex. I be watching the door. I could see her shadow by the door."

"Cut it out, Kandice. It be dark in the hallway. How can you see a shadow in the dark?"

"Whatever. She acts like she likes me when you're around but once you leave, she gives me so much attitude. Just like you didn't believe me when I told you she set me up in Victoria's Secret. It was her who put those panties in my bag. What the hell I look like stealing a pair of panties? A size small anyway. I was in there begging and pleading with the manager not to call the cops. I had to convince her that they slipped in my bag by mistake."

"I'll talk to her, alright, baby?"

"Ok, but I'm not coming over there again until you do. I'm not ready to die just yet," she said.

"Alright, I'm on my way."

******

I pulled up to the office and got out the car. At the same time, police cars were pulling up to the office as well. I stopped in front of the door.

"Can I help y'all?" I asked them.

"We have an arrest warrant for a Kandice Marie Jackson. We were informed that she's employed here, and you are, sir?" the one officer asked.

"I'm the owner."

"Ok, so then you should be a pretty smart man. Smart enough to know what happens when you interfere with apprehension of a suspect." I rolled my eyes and unlocked the door. They were going to get in whether I allowed them to or not.

I walked in first and they followed behind me. I got into the office and Kandi jumped up out of the chair with excitement, until she saw the officers behind me.

"What's going on?" she asked.

"Ma'am, are you Kandice Marie Jackson?" the officer asked.

"Yes, I am. What's this about?"

"You're under arrest for the assault on Thomas Hanes."

"Who the hell is Thomas Hanes?" I asked.

"June," she said.

"Shit, I'll get you a lawyer. Don't worry about nothing."

They handcuffed her and walked her straight out the building. I hopped in my car and followed them down to the precinct. I wanted to make sure she got down there safe. I didn't trust those fucking cops. I picked up the phone and called my pops.

"Pops, I need you to send Joel down to the precinct. I'm willing to pay whatever, I just need him immediately," I said.

"Ok, son," he said, hanging up the phone.

Five minutes later, my father was calling me back.

"Joel is on his way. You want to tell me what's going on now?" he asked.

"They arrested Kandice on assault charges."

"Who the hell did my daughter-in-law assault?" my father asked. In the last few weeks, he fell in love with Kandice and Kianni. So much so he started calling her daughter-in-law, and Kandice and I weren't really official just yet.

"Her old boss. She stabbed his ass after he tried to rape her."

"Oh, damn. I'm going to call ya brother, we're on our way down there," he said hanging up the phone. I sat outside the precinct pacing back and forth, waiting on Joel to come. When he finally did arrive, he walked up to me.

"Tell me what's going on," he said. No hi or nothing, just straight to business; that's what I liked. I ran down the story to him.

"Alright, let's go," he said, walking ahead of me. I waited in the lobby for him to come back out. I felt like I was waiting forever. When he walked back out, I ran up to him.

"How is she? What's going to happen? Can I post bail?" I

said, bombarding him with questions.

"She's doing good. She's a G as you guys say it. We won't know about bail until she's in front of a judge tomorrow morning. I'm going to have her enter a plea of self-defense. As of now, all you can do is go home and get some rest and be at the court tomorrow." My brother and father came running in just as Joel and I were turning to leave.

"What the hell happened?" Tech asked when he reached us.

"Kandice was arrested for stabbing her boss—who tried to rape her—in the ribs with a pen," I said.

"Wait, like an ink pen?" Tech asked.

"Yes, an ink pen. And now this pussy nigga trying to press charges on her. Joel is going to have her plead self-defense and hopefully I can post bail for her tomorrow."

Once I was done talking with them, we all went our separate ways. I called Saniyah and had her take Kianni to her house for the night. I went back to the office and shut everything down and locked up. I was getting in my car when I heard a loud ass explosion. One after another. I reached in my car for my gun and slowly walked toward the direction of the explosion. I walked over to the garage, put in the code, and as soon as the doors opened, a blaze of fire exploded out.

"Fuck!" I yelled as I stood back and watched my garage with a few of my buses go up in flames. This was not my fucking day at all. I pulled out my phone and called 911, followed by my insurance company. Somebody was gonna pay for this shit.

It was three in the morning when I finally got home and was able to lay my head back. I was exhausted and just ready to go to bed and wake up and get Kandice out of jail. I kicked off my jeans and pulled off my shirt, and laid there in nothing but my boxers.

As my mind raced replaying today's events, I started slowly drifting off into a deep sleep. I was having a dream that I was getting some good ass head from someone, but the room I was in was dark so I couldn't see their face. The shit felt real. A little too real. I slowly opened my eyes realizing that I wasn't dreaming. Someone was really giving me head, but the room was dark and I couldn't see a face. I wanted to stop the person but the shit felt so good. After this person started swirling their tongue around my dick, I knew exactly who it was. I pushed her off the bed and jumped off it, and ran to wall and cut the lights on.

"Kori, what the fuck do you think you're doing?" I asked.

"What I used to do for you, baby," she said, sitting on the bed.

"Nah, get the fuck up and get out my room," I said to her.

"Did I do something wrong? Is this about that Kandice girl you think you're into?"

"I don't think anything. I know I'm into her and after tomorrow, I'm moving her and her son in and you gotta go, baby girl. Your parents have been dying to know how you are doing. I'm sure they'll take you in and get you the help that you need."

"Wait, so you're putting me out, Johnathan? This bitch comes in the picture and you're ready to toss me out on the streets, Johnathan? I thought we had more? You promised me that if I got clean we could work things out. I know you're with her but if you send me to my parents' house, I know I'm going to relapse. Johnathan, please don't do this," she begged and pleaded. I've always had a weakness for Kori. She was my high school love. But I think I had more of a weakness for Kandice, and I knew if Kori was still living here, Kandice would never agree to move in with me.

"Come on, Johnathan. I just need a few more months where I can completely be clean and be able to get a job and get out of your hair."

"Let me ask you this and depending on your answer, I'll let you stay for a few more weeks. Did you put them underwear inside of Kandice's bag at Victoria's Secret?" She sat there for a minute.

"Yes, I don't like seeing you with her. I never thought you'd move on. You were making promises that we would get together once I got clean. Now you out here playing family man with this chick. What about me?" she asked.

"What about you? I gave you too many chances for you to get clean and you never did. Now it's just a little too late. I found someone else. You have to find a way to move on. I'm sorry to have to say that to you, but you hurt me bad, Kori. Now I've found someone who treats me great, was just like you and was able to come through, and look how many times it took me to help you before you actually gave in. I'll let you stay here for a little while longer, but you're going to have to go pretty soon or you're going to just have to deal with the fact that I'm going to be with Kandice. She's perfect."

"No one's perfect, Johnathan," she said, walking out the room and slamming the door.

I got back in bed and just laid there for the next few hours. I was able to get a lot of thinking done. I think I pretty much knew who set my garage on fire. I got out the bed and went to take a shower. I got dress and was down at the courthouse, waiting for the shit to open.

Kandi

"I can't believe this shit is happening right now," I said to myself, as I paced back and forth in the holding room, waiting to be called to see the judge. I was really hoping they accepted the self-defense plea and released me on bail. I had a good 25 grand in the floorboard of my apartment and about 800 in my bank account. I had something for that fucker June. He wanted to press charges, I'm about to ruin that nigga's whole life.

"Jackson," one of the officers called.

"I'm here," I called, running to the opening of the holding cell. I was taken upstairs to the courtroom. As soon as I entered the courtroom, the first person I spotted was my lawyer. He came walking up to the front of the room, holding a folder. Then I saw Johnathan sitting there looking like he hadn't slept in years. He smiled and waved at me and I did the same. He walked up closer to the front and sat in the front row.

"Ms. Jackson, you're here for the aggravated assault of Mr. Hanes. How do you plead?" the judge asked lazily. He looked as if he was still asleep. I guess my case bored his ass. Good, maybe he'll let my ass go.

"Your Honor, my client would like to plead not guilty by reason of self-defense. My client was only trying to protect herself against Mr. Hanes, who had become physically aggressive with her. We have a witness who can attest previous incidents where Mr. Hanes had become physical with my client. We also have a witness who can testify to seeing my client, Ms. Jackson, running out of the office of Mr. Hanes on the night of the incident, in tears. We ask that Ms. Jackson be released on bail. She's a single parent with no one to care for her child. She's not a flight risk and she has less than one thousand dollars in her savings account and no profitable assets," my lawyers spoke. After hearing him talk his talk, I was for sure my ass was getting up out this bitch. He was good. I don't know how or where he got witnesses and access to my bank accounts, but I didn't give a fuck as long as he could get me home to my baby. The judge sat there reading over what I assumed was my file, and then put it down and looked over at me.

"Ms. Jackson, did you really stab that man with a pen?" he asked. I looked over at my lawyer to see how to answer the question, and he just nodded his head 'yes' to go on and answer.

"Yes, your honor, but it was only out of protection of me. I am not a violent person. It was the only—" I said and he held up his hand.

"Wow, I'm sure that took a lot strength," he laughed.

"Bail is granted," he said, banging his gavel. I was happy as hell to hear that. I turned towards Johnathan.

"I have money in one of the floorboards at my house, in my room under the dresser. You can get the key from Saniyah," I

213

said.

"Girl, shut up. I got you, Ma. Save your money, you worked hard for that. I'm going to go post it now. I'll see you in a few," he said, walking out the courtroom.

An hour later, I was being released. I ran up out that shit like Madea did in her movie *Madea Goes to Jail*. I walked up to Johnathan and kissed him on the lips.

"You know we do too much kissing for you not to be my girl yet," he said.

"Wait, so this whole time I wasn't your girl?" I joked.

"Damn, and here I was curving niggas like I had a man when I could have been doing my thing."

"What thing? Don't make me hurt you," he said, opening the door for me to get in the car.

"Does Tech still talk to Pepper? I need a favor from her," I said.

"I don't know. He hasn't mentioned her in a while. Last thing he said about her was that she burned the skin off his dick."

"Ewe, she burned him?"

"Not burn like that, crazy. Like literally burned him, with fire," he said. I couldn't stop laughing. That shit was funny. I could always tell Pepper had a few screws loose just by her performances alone.

"Yea, Pepper is a wild girl."

Chapter 18

Kori

I sat on the balcony, smoking a cigarette. I wasn't allowed to smoke in the house anymore because that bitch didn't like the smell. Since the night Johnathan told me he wasn't trying to get back with me, I have been sheltered up in my room. I had isolated myself to my room. I didn't care what he said, he was going to be my man again one way or another. I put my cigarette out and walked back into the house. I walked down the hall and entered Johnathan's room. I started going through his drawers, and then his closet. I became disgusted at the sight of a few of Kandice's clothes hanging up next to his. I started ripping them down off the hangers like the crazy woman I was. I noticed in the back of the closet, he had one an old school 76ers jersey hanging up. He wore this on our first date back in high school. I found myself becoming filled with emotions, memories, and flashback of him and I.

We were so in love and everyone said we made a great couple. Everybody loved them some Korina and Johnathan. He and I flooded the class of 2007 yearbook. He was voted most athletic, class clown and best dressed. I was voted most likely to succeed, best smile, and both of us were voted best looking, and that we were. Before the drugs, I was drop dead gorgeous. I stood 5'6, 120 pounds, yellow bone, long pretty hair, and green eyes. I was biracial, mixed with white from my father, and Nigerian from my mother. I just knew he and I were going to make some pretty ass babies, but I ruined that when I started using. Johnathan loved me to death and no matter how many times people told him something was right about me, he never believed them. He was in denial for a long time, until the hospital confirmed what everyone had been saying. I really hurt that man and all I wanted was a chance to do it over again.

I took the jersey off the hanger and walked out the closet with it. I went to his dresser and sprayed his cologne on it, and curled up in the bed with it and closed my eyes. I heard a car door shut and I jumped up and ran to the window. It was the bitch. I left out the room and stood at the entrance door of my bedroom.

"Yea babe, I'm here. Where did you say your sneakers were?" I heard her coming into the house. She started walking up the stairs and stopped, and picked up a pair of Johnathan's basketball sneakers that he left on the top of the staircase.

217

"Alright, I got them. See you in a bit, baby," she said, hanging up the phone.

I really hated this bitch. Just as she turned to go back down the stairs, I ran from out of my room that was next to the staircase and I pushed her down the stairs. I stood at the top and just watched as her body rolled down the steps, finally coming to stop at the bottom. She laid there motionless. I prayed she was dead, but after checking her pulse, she wasn't. I thought about finishing her off, but I wanted to make her suffer. I ran upstairs to my room and moved my dresser from near the wall. I pulled out my stash box that I kept there for a rainy day. There was a moment when I almost had a slip but I remember the night I walked in on John and Kandi fucking and had to remember my reason for getting clean. I sat on the bed prepped the needle and heroine then ran back downstairs. She was still passed out so I grabbed her arm and injected her with the drug. When I was done, I dragged her back up the stairs to my room. This bitch was heavy as hell. I really had to struggle to get her up the stairs. I tied her hands and feet together and stuffed and taped up her mouth. I dragged her deep into my closet and shut the door. My next move was to get rid of her car. I had to make it so that it would seem as though she came and left. I wasn't going to kill her, I was going to make Johnathan think she disappeared on him and then he and I would be able to be together.

Chapter 20

Two weeks

Johnathan

"Yo Pops, you heard from ya guy yet?" I asked my father.

"Nah, son, nothing yet. I told you when I do, I'll give you call. You're going to drive yourself crazy thinking about that girl. How do you know she ain't just pick up and leave? She does have that court hearing come up."

"Because, Pops, she wouldn't do that. She wouldn't leave her son like that for two weeks straight. If there is one thing I know about Kandice, she's a great mother and she would never do some shit like that. Somebody did something to her or has her. I know it, Pops, I feel it in my bones."

"Have they located her car yet?" he asked.

"Nah, not yet. But they can't do anything because her car was sold. It didn't have GPS, so all they can do is put a BOLO on it."

"Damn, well alright, son. I'll keep you updated if Billy finds any information," my father said as we hung up. I set my phone on the table and sat my head back on the couch. It had been two whole weeks exactly since Kandice had gone missing. The last time I spoke to her, she had come to the house to pick up my sneakers for me. She said she had them and was on her way back, but she never showed up. My dad was a bounty hunter back in the day and he still takes jobs every now and then. He got one of the guys he knows to help look for Kandice, but they've been coming up empty handed. They even got in touch with her parents and they hadn't seen her either. I reached for my phone again and called Saniyah's phone. I wanted to speak with Kianni before he went to bed.

"Hey, Saniyah, how's Kianni doing?" I asked.

"Ok, I guess. He keeps asking about his mommy," she said.

"Ok, let me speak to him, please." She handed him the phone.

"Hey, little man, what's going on?" I asked.

"Hi, Coach John. Did my mommy come home yet?"

"No buddy, she's still on vacation," I lied. I couldn't tell him his mom was missing but then again, it would have been better than telling him she's dead or that she ran away and left him here without a mommy.

"When is she coming home?"

"Soon, I promise." Just the sound of his voice broke my heart. I talked to him a little longer before it was time for him to go to bed. I hung up with him just as Kori came in with a plate of food and set it on the table.

"Have you heard anything from her yet?" she asked.

"Nah, not yet," I answered.

"I may not have liked her, but I do feel bad, because she has a son. I really hope you find her," she said, walking back into the kitchen. Lately, Kori had really been stepping up. She has been clean for some time now. The antibiotics have been helping her skin clear up and she started gaining her weight back and her hair started growing again. It was nice seeing her look like her old self again.

I picked up the fork and started eating the spaghetti she cooked. When I was done, I went and showered and laid down. I haven't slept in days, so I doubt if I would have been able to sleep tonight. I laid there going through my phone. There was a knock at the door and I knew it was Kori.

"Yea, come in," I called and she opened the door.

"Hey," she said walking into the bedroom.

"What's up, Kori?" I asked, never taking my eyes off the phone.

"Nothing, just wanted to check on you and make sure you're ok," she said, sitting down on the bed.

"I'm good, you good?" I asked.

"Yea, I'm doing great. Is there something I can get for you, or do for you?" she asked, putting her hand on my thigh, moving it up towards my dick.

"No, I'm good," I said.

"You sure?" she asked, now with her hand resting on my dick.

"I'm good, Kori, you can go now," I said, moving her hand off me.

"Why are you acting like that, Johnathan?" she whined, grabbing for my dick again. I smacked her hands away again.

"Kori, get the hell out. I told you we have nothing anymore. I'm happy you got clean but you know the deal already," I said to her.

"I got clean for you, Johnathan, and you acting like this? Do you know how hard it is trying to kick this habit? Do you know the pain I endured going through withdrawals? Do you have any idea how hard it is trying not to stick that needle in my arm instead of—" she said, stopping herself.

"You know, I did it for you so all that doesn't matter."

"That's your problem right there. You did it for me, not for yourself, Korina. Kandice kicked the habit for herself and she got better for herself, not for no man. That's the difference between the two of you. I love you, Korina, but I'm in love with Kandice," I said. She looked at me with tears in her eyes.

"Fuck Kandice," she said, walking out the room. I sat up in bed with my head hung low. I never wanted to hurt Kori, but she hurt me so many times there's no way I could ever trust her with my heart again. I got up out of bed and started putting some clothes on. I needed to get out the house. I called Tech to let him know I was on my way over.

****

When I got to Tech's house, I could hear the music and

smell the weed all the way outside the door. I knocked and walked straight in like I always did. He, Pepper, and her stripper friend, Keisha, were sitting on the couch.

"What up y'all?" I asked, as I plopped down on the couch.

"Hey, bro, how you doing?" Tech asked. I shrugged my shoulder.

"I'm cool, I guess. I thought y'all two wasn't together anymore," I said to him and Pepper.

"Please, you know your brother can't leave me alone," Pepper said. And Tech shook his head.

"Yea, you know this my baby right here. Best head I've ever had in my life."

"That's right, momma knows how to treat her daddy," she said, reaching over and giving Tech a kiss on the lips. A little too much. They were sitting there, sucking and slobbing each other down.

"Take that shit in the room," I called. They both jumped up from the couch, running into the bedroom. I stood up from the couch and reached for the remote to change the channel.

225

"How you know I wasn't watching that?" Keisha asked.

"I'm sorry, were you?"

"No, but I could have been," she said. I looked at her and then back at the television screen.

"I'm sorry to hear about Kandi."

"You didn't even like Kandice so save it," I said, never taking my eyes off the TV.

"That's true I don't like her, but I would never wish any harm to come her way, even though she fucked my shit all up," she said, referring to the night Kandice whooped her ass outside the club. I laughed because Kandice did fuck her shit up.

"You gotta have hands to back up that shit talking, Ma," I said as I continued to look through the channel. Keisha lit one of the blunts up and started smoking it.

"Wanna hit?" she asked, holding the blunt out towards me.

"Yea, give me that," I replied, taking it from her, putting it in my mouth and pulling it.

"Good, right?" Keisha asked. I shook my head and passed it back to her.

Keisha and I sat there passing the blunt back and forth and watching *Wolf of Wall Street*. It was going on an hour and Tech and Pepper were still in there going at it.

I sat back on the couch with my hands behind my head, watching the movie. I was higher than a damn kite. During our puff-puff-pass session, I had moved over to the same couch as Keisha. She was laid back, chilling and laughing at the movie. I felt myself drifting off to sleep. I guess it was from the weed. I haven't slept in days, so I embraced the sleep as it came. I jumped up at the touch of someone's hands down my sweats. I opened my eyes and Keisha was hovering over me. It was like she was moving in slow motion as I laid there. She pulled my dick out my shorts and put it in her mouth. I don't know what the fuck was with these women wanting to shove my dick in their mouth. She started sucking and slurping on my shit like the expert she was. I wanted to stop her, but it was feeling too good. The weed had completely taken over my body, because I couldn't move or nothing, and the feel of her warm, wet mouth was everything I needed at the moment. I grabbed on to her hair and started guiding her head up and down every now and then, pushing it further down her throat. I guess she wasn't the expert I thought she was because she gagged every time. This was nothing like Kandi, but it still felt good. I felt my phone start to vibrate. I answered the phone without really looking at the screen.

"Who told you to stop?" I said to Keisha who had suddenly stopped what she was doing. When I said that, she went back to doing what she was doing.

"Hello," I answered.

"Hi, I'm calling because I found a young lady here in the alley. She looks like she's in bad shape. I believe it's drugs she's on. I found her phone near and your number was the last she called." Hearing the word needle, I assumed it was Kori, but Kori didn't own a cell phone. I removed the phone from my ear and checked the name; it was Kandi.

"Oh shit. Get off me," I said, pushing Keisha to the living room floor. She hit her head on the leg of the coffee table.

"Damn, nigga," she said, rubbing the back of her head.

"Where are you?" I asked the man on the other end of the phone. He sent me the address and I ran to get Tech without even knocking on the door. When I got in the room, I had to rub my eyes to make sure I was seeing what the fuck I was seeing. My brother's hands and feet were individually tied up to the bedpost, and Pepper was standing over him naked with a bottle of baby oil and a torch lighter.

"What the fuck is going on in here? You know what—I don't even wanna know. Yo, I think I found Kandi," I said. Tech spit the balled up cloth he had in his mouth out.

"Ok nigga, but why is your dick out?" he asked. I looked down. I forgot to put it away.

"I was using the bathroom. Yo psycho, untie my brother," I said to Pepper, as I ran out the room and out the apartment.

Chapter 21

Kandi

I opened my eyes and the room was blurry. Wherever I was quiet and the only thing that could be heard was beeping. I rubbed at my eyes trying to get some sort of vision. Looking around, I could now see that I was in a hospital. The last thing I remember was being pushed down the stairs and then waking up and being tied up and blindfolded, and being stuck with needles and then passing out again. I knew it was Kori who did it. Every time I woke up, I would hear her voice. I was going to murder that bitch as soon as I got out this hospital. I tried moving my legs but they were restricted by something hard and heavy. I removed the blanket that was covering my legs and they both had casts on them.

"Damn," I said just as the door came open. I looked up to my dad and Kianni.

"Mommy," Kianni said, running to my bed. I gasped for air as tears started streaming down my eyes. He jumped on the bed, and I grabbed him and squeezed him so tight.

"Oh my God, I missed you so much, baby," I said to him.

"I missed you too, Mommy," he said. I let him go and cupped his face and just looked at him.

"Mommy, how come you didn't take me on the trip with you?" he asked. I looked up at my father and he gave me a wink.

"Because it was a Mommy's trip, baby. Next time you can come on the trip with me, ok?" He shook his head.

"Hey, Dad," I said and he came over and gave me a hug.

"How you feeling?" he asked me.

"Confused and hungry. How long was I in here?"

"Four days, but you been on vacation for two weeks," he said, looking down at Kianni.

"Has Johnathan been here?" I asked.

"Not yet today, but he was here yesterday," he said and I shook my head.

"Where's your wife? She let you come see me?"

"Your mother and I separated, baby. We have been for

about a year. There's been something going on that I've been wanting to talk to you about," he said, just as a strange guy knocked on the door and came in.

"You're back. Kandice, this is my friend, Edward. Edward, this is my daughter, Kandice," my father said.

"Nice to finally meet you. I've heard many nice things about you," he said, shaking my hand. Just by the switch alone I knew exactly who this was. My father had finally come out that damn closet.

"Nice to meet you too, Edward."

"Here you go, little man," Edward said, handing Kianni a McDonald's bag.

"Aye, what I tell you about eating that stuff," I said to Kianni.

"But I was hungry, Mommy."

"Hey, you tricked me. I thought you said Mommy lets you eat McDonald's," my dad said. Kianni just looked at me and smiled. I heard the door open up again and in walked Johnathan.

"Hey, you," I said as he walked in.

"Hey, yourself," he said, walking up to the bed and kissing me on the forehead.

"How you feeling?"

"I'm feeling good," I lied. I wasn't feeling good at all. I was getting this familiar itch that I felt like I needed to scratch. Johnathan went and sat down in the chair in the corner of the room. He didn't seem too excited to see me. The whole time he just sat there on his phone, not saying anything unless someone spoke to him. I wasn't feeling the shit at all.

"You know, if there's something else you would rather be doing or somewhere you'd be, you can go," I said calmly. He looked up from his phone and at me to see who I was talking too.

"You talking to me?" he asked.

"Uh, yes I am. What the hell is your problem?"

"How about we go get some cookies?" my father said, taking Kianni off the bed, and the three of them left the room.

"What's my problem, Kandice? Yo' ass was gone for two weeks and some man found yo' ass high ass a fucking kite,

233

Kandice. Do you know how crazy I went looking for you? I had my dad and a fucking search team out looking for you, Kandice. I had to lie to Kianni and tell him you were on vacation. That little boy cried asking me why you didn't want to take him with you, because you decided to jump back on that white horse, Kandice. That's my fucking problem. What the fuck is it with you women and that fucking drug? I bet you got the itch right now for that shit. I'm not dealing with the shit, Kandice. I dealt with my ex for years, I'm done with it. You and her could get lost and high together and leave me the fuck alone," he yelled. He was really mad. Not once since I had been talking to him had he ever yelled at anyone.

"What the hell is you crying for? Wipe ya damn face," he said, throwing the tissue box on the bed. I hadn't realized how bad I was crying until he mentioned it. When did I become a cry baby? I hardly ever cried and definitely never cried when someone yelled at me.

"It was Kori," I said through my tears.

"What?" he asked, which made me cry even harder.

"What the hell is you crying for, Kandice? What did you just say?"

"I said it was Kori."

"What do you mean it was Kori?"

"When I went to the house to get your sneakers, she pushed me down the stairs. When I woke up, I was tied up, blindfolded, and gagged. Every day she pushed those needles in my arm, four maybe five times a day. She did this to me. After all these years, you think I would jump back on the needle like that? I could barely take the sight of Kori when you found her passed out, or when she had her withdrawal moments. Seeing that brought back so many unwanted memories and regrets. If you don't respect me as a person, then respect me as a mother and know that I would never intentionally leave my son for a few days, let alone a few weeks. Your ex bitch did this to me after I warned you about her ass. The bitch tried to poison me with bleach. You still think she wouldn't hurt a fly, Johnathan, huh? Well, the bitch broke both of my legs and polluted my body with that mess I worked so hard to kick," I said, crying all over again. Johnathan stood there silently. He went back and sat in the chair he was in, before pulling out his phone.

"Tech, I need you to meet me at my house as soon as possible. It's an emergency," he said, hanging up. He stood up

235

from the chair and walked over to me and sat on the bed. He cupped my chin.

"I'm so sorry she did this to you and I'm sorry for yelling. I was just really worried and scared. I didn't know what could have happened to you. I was going out of my damn mind, but I promise you, you won't have to worry about Kori, I'm going to handle it, ok?"

"Ok," I said, shaking my head up and down.

Johnathan

I raced out of the hospital and jumped in my car. I couldn't believe Kori could have done this shit to Kandice. I knew she was in love with me, but I didn't think she was capable of physically harming another human being. I raced to my house which wasn't too far away. I had called Tech so he could meet me there to prevent me from choking her to death when I confronted her, but he didn't answer the phone. I left a message telling him to meet me here; hopefully, he showed up. I pulled up to the house and jumped out the car.

"Kori," I yelled as I stormed into the house. It was quiet and a little eerie.

"Kori," I yelled again and no answer. I ran up the stairs and into her room. I looked in the bathroom and she wasn't in there either. I walked back out the room.

"Kori," I yelled again before I felt a sharp pain in my back. I tried reaching for it but couldn't. I turn around and Kori stood there with a butcher knife in her hand. She lunged at me with the knife, this time jabbing it in my chest. I grabbed onto my chest as I fell to the ground. She sat on top of me and drove the knife in me again and again in different locations. She stood above me as I struggled to breathe.

"If I can't have you, no one will," she said, as she drove the knife into her own chest.

To Be Continued...

Other Releases from Myiesha:

A New Jersey Love Story: Troy & Camilla

A New Jersey Love Story 2: I Got Yours, You Got Mine

A New Jersey Love Story 3: Bulletproof Love

A New Jersey Love Story 4: The Finale

Knight in Chrome: Knight & Blaize

Knight in Chrome Armor 2: Blaized Obsession

Knight in Chrome Armor 3: A Chivalrous Ending

Disturbed: An Unbalanced Love

Thank you so much for your support

With Love,

Myiesha S. Mason

Please leave your reviews on what you thought of the book

Also you can follow me on Facebook at

Myiesha Mason

Or Instagram at

_miss_mason

Or contact me through email at

myieshasharaemason@gmail.com

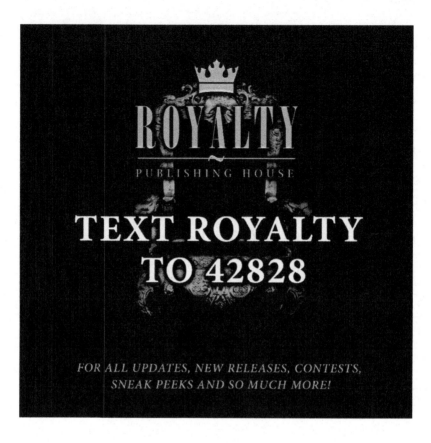

Looking for a publishing home?

Royalty Publishing House, Where the Royals reside, is accepting submissions for writers in the urban fiction genre. If you're interested, submit the first 3-4 chapters with your synopsis to submissions@royaltypublishinghouse.com.

Check out our website for more information:

www.royaltypublishinghouse.com.

Be sure to LIKE our Royalty Publishing House page

on Facebook

COMING NEXT...

Did you grab our last #Royal release?

Do You Like CELEBRITY GOSSIP? Check Out

QUEEN DYNASTY!

Like Our Page HERE! Visit Our Site:

www.thequeendynasty.com

HAVE YOU CLICKED ON THESE

RELEASES?

Royalty Publishing House

Young
LOVE IN
Memphis 3
Heart On Reserve

B. LOVE

Royal Release

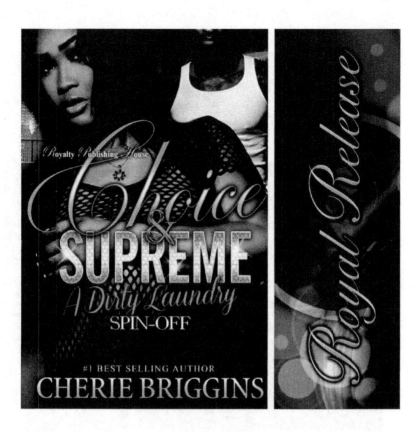

Royalty Publishing House

Choice
&
SUPREME
A Dirty Laundry
SPIN-OFF

#1 BEST SELLING AUTHOR
CHERIE BRIGGINS

Royal Release

He's Nothing Like Them Other Ones
Myiesha

CPSIA information can be obtained
at www.ICGtesting.com
Printed in the USA
LVOW04s2126230117
521885LV00017B/783/P

9 781540 722522